LADYKILLER

Maya put an arm around her husband's shoulders and said miserably, "Murder, Bernard."

"Yes."

"Murder . . . and Snooky."

Bernard looked at his wife's drawn, anxious face. "Have they considered suicide?" he asked gently.

"Suicide?" She gave him a questioning look. "No. I don't know. Why should they?"

"I just thought the woman might have killed herself in order to get out of the date with Snooky."

"Bernard, that's not funny. Snooky's usually very successful with women. There's something about him that makes women want to mother him."

But Bernard had lost interest in Snooky. He was gazing out the window with a contemplative, faraway look in his eyes. "Murder," he said softly.

Bantam Crime Line Books offer the finest
in classic and modern American mysteries
Ask your bookseller for the books you have missed

GLORIA DANK

GOING OUT IN STYLE

BANTAM BOOKS
NEW YORK · TORONTO · LONDON · SYDNEY · AUCKLAND

GOING OUT IN STYLE
A Bantam Book / January 1990

ISBN 0-553-28346-4

Published simultaneously in the United States and Canada

Bantam Books are published by Bantam Books, a division of Bantam Doubleday
Dell Publishing Group, Inc. Its trademark, consisting of the words "Bantam
Books" and the portrayal of a rooster, is Registered in U.S. Patent and
Trademark Office and in other countries. Marca Registrada. Bantam Books,
666 Fifth Avenue, New York, New York 10103.

PRINTED IN THE UNITED STATES OF AMERICA

OPM   0 9 8 7 6 5 4 3 2 1

To Jacob

1

Bella Whitaker gazed upon her reflection in the mirror with profound self-satisfaction. "As good-looking as ever, you old broad," she thought, twirling to show off her long dress with the flared skirt. She was dressed up for an evening on the town: long black dress, black stockings, and spiky black heels. On her neck and ears and wrists glittered her gorgeous diamond-and-sapphire set, the one that her husband Charles ("God rest his soul," she thought) had bought her years ago. She considered the tiara, but decided that it was too much; enough was enough, even if she *was* going into Manhattan, a rare enough occurrence these days. She leaned closer to the mirror; up close, a network of lines could be seen cobwebbing her face under the makeup, but farther back and in the right light she could be mistaken for, say, forty of her sixty-eight years. Her hair was a rather determined shade of auburn—she could never bear the idea of going gray—and her eyes were as beautiful and vibrant as ever, unusual in their mixture of green and blue. "As good-looking as ever," she

whispered to herself, and swept downstairs to snatch up her black mink.

It is a sad but true fact that so many of our day-to-day thoughts tend to be ordinary, even banal. As it was, Bella Whitaker was proceeding in her rapid yet majestic way toward the front door of her Connecticut home, her black dress trailing behind her, and her mind was fully occupied with thoughts of the salmon steak she planned to order that evening—she was even toying with the idea of ordering that morel mushroom sauce with it, she loved mushrooms—when someone quite well known to her slipped up behind her and put a rope around her neck.

Philippe Bergère was worried. He was, in fact, extremely worried, on the point of becoming actually agitated. It was nine-fifteen on a Friday evening—one of his *busiest* evenings of the week—and Mrs. Whitaker had not yet arrived. It was, he thought frostily, an outrage—an insult—*quelle horreur—insupportable* . . . and various other things, which he expressed to himself indignantly in French but mostly in English, since his repertoire of French words was distinctly limited. Philippe Bergère, the maître d' of the most fashionable and trendy new restaurant on Manhattan's fashionable and trendy Upper East Side, was not actually French; not *strictly* French, as he liked to put it to himself, although his grandfather had been undoubtedly French and he himself had spent quite a lot of time in Montreal. Nevertheless, the upper-class patrons of Le Roi Soleil need not know that, and Philippe himself was so overcome with his role as conductor of what he regarded as a vast food symphony that he often quite genuinely forgot that English was his mother tongue. Now, in his extreme agitation, was one of those times.

He swept down upon the young man nursing his drink in a corner of the bar.

"M'sieu—m'sieu, you must pardon me, but we need the table, you understand! It is Friday night, one of my busiest nights, m'sieu! I am, how you say, *désolé*, but there is nothing I can do for you. I must, I simply *must* have the table!" In his excitement he spoke all in exclamation points.

The young man looked up and smiled. It was a genuinely affable smile, spreading across his lean intelligent face. He had straight golden-brown hair which fell across his forehead, a thin crooked nose and light brown eyes. Now he waved an indolent hand and said, "Please, please, Philippe, don't bother yourself. It's no problem at all. I'll wait here, and when Mrs. Whitaker arrives, you give me a whistle, okay?"

"Yes, m'sieu," the maître d' said meekly. Inside he bristled. Who was this little nobody from nowhere who dared to refer to him, Philippe Bergère, by his first name, as if they had met before? Who was he, who dared to ask the maître d' of the finest restaurant on the Upper East Side to, he thought painfully, "give him a whistle"? The part of him which had once, before this incarnation, been just plain Philip Berger, growing up on the streets of Brooklyn, knew perfectly well what "give a whistle" meant; but the part which was Philippe Bergère did not, how you say, comprehend it. He bristled inwardly and said stiffly again, "Yes, yes," before bustling away toward his more important clientele.

The young man brushed his hair out of his eyes, glanced at his watch and ordered another drink. He was not drinking anything alcoholic because on an empty stomach that always made him sick. His order remained the same— Perrier with lime—throughout the evening, but as time wore on his stomach became more and more painfully empty. He went to the phone twice to make a call, but each time there was no answer and he returned to his seat, where he sat quietly, sipping his drink and listening to the conversations around him. Now and again a brilliant smile lit up his face as he overheard something that amused him.

At eleven-fifteen he looked at his watch, shrugged, and went to get his coat. On his way out the door he passed by the maître d'.

"So long, Philippe," he said. "Great evening. *Merci bien, et la prochaine fois vous devez me promettre de parler seulement en français, hein?*"

The maitre d' stared indignantly after him. Definitely, he thought . . . definitely, he should not encourage these *plaisanteries* . . . he should not let these little nobodies into his restaurant.

*   *   *

It was a two-hour drive back to his sister's house in Ridgewood, Connecticut, and when he got there the young man went straight up to the third-floor guest room and, falling into bed, slept soundly for ten hours. It was nearly noon before there was a soft knock on his door.

"Aaauuuurrgghhh," he said from under the blankets. "Go 'way. Leave me alone. I'm asleep."

The door opened and a person who looked just like himself, but female and a bit older, came in. She sat down on the edge of his bed and regarded him impassively.

"The little birdies are all awake, Snookers. They woke up seven hours ago. What about you?"

"Go 'way. Leave me alone."

"I remember when you were a little boy," his sister said. "Much shorter and cuter than you are now. Every morning you'd sleep through the alarm, and I'd have to come in and drag you out of bed and get you ready for school. How I loved those days. William would stand at the foot of the stairs bellowing something about how you were a slothful toad, and I'd be screaming and dragging you out of bed by the collar of your pajamas. I'd feed you and make sure you were dressed properly, all in two minutes flat." She sighed. "Those were fun days, weren't they, Snooky? Special days. Silly of me to think they were all over when you went away to college."

"Go 'way," said her brother stubbornly from beneath the pillow. "Leave me alone."

Maya regarded the inert mass beneath the blankets and her face lit up with an enchanting smile. She looked just like her brother: the same straight golden-brown hair, crooked elegant nose, pale face and rangy build. He was in his mid twenties and she was five years older, but otherwise they could have passed as twins.

"How was your date last night?"

Snooky Randolph opened one eye. "It wasn't. It didn't happen. She didn't show. Okay? Feel free to laugh at me."

"I won't laugh. Poor Snooky. Did you wait all evening?"

"Yes. And why? Because I'm an idiot." He slouched down farther under the covers. "I have no luck with women."

Maya regarded him soberly. He had arrived on her doorstep fresh from a painful breakup with a woman he had been living with in California. "Don't let it get to you, Snookers."

"I can't help it. It's depressing, it really is. My male ego is on the line. I'm shaky . . . vulnerable. . . ." He sighed and moved restlessly underneath the covers. "I don't know how to describe it."

"Pathetic?"

"Yes, Maya. Pathetic. That's the right word. That's what I am. A shattered wreck of a formerly joyful human being."

"You were never joyful. Were you?"

"I think so," said Snooky. He moved his head restlessly on the pillow. "Wasn't I? I can't remember anymore. I can't remember anything that happened before a few weeks ago."

"Poor Snooky."

He sat up. His face looked sleepy and vulnerable, making him look, Maya thought with a pang, terribly young. Not so different from the seven-year-old she had shaken out of bed all those years ago. He rubbed his eyes, looked foggily out the window and said, "Cold in here, isn't it?"

"It's freezing."

"Bernard?"

"Yes."

They often talked this way, in verbal shorthand. Now Snooky nodded and yawned. "Okay." He got up, draped the blankets around him, and wandered out in the direction of the bathroom. Maya shivered, pulling her sweater tightly around her. She glanced around the guest room, with its hardwood floor, antique bedstead, and sloping timbered ceiling. Her husband Bernard kept the third floor at subzero temperatures throughout the winter. He claimed that this was to save on heating bills, but the real reason was to discourage guests from staying very long. Snooky accepted this, as he had accepted everything about Bernard from the day five years ago when he had met him. "Bernard's crazy about me," he often confided to his sister, "absolutely crazy about me."

"It's true, Snooks. He does say you make him crazy."

"You know what I mean."

Now she got to her feet, called "See you downstairs," and went down to rejoin her husband at the breakfast table.

When Snooky slouched downstairs fifteen minutes later he went into the kitchen and made himself a plate of scrambled eggs and toast. Then he sat down at the broad mahogany dining room table and eyed his brother-in-law warily.

"Can I ask you a question, Bernard?"

Bernard was eating his way steadily through an enormous pile of flapjacks smothered in syrup. "No."

"Why in the world is the third floor freezing cold?"

Bernard regarded him sullenly. "Because nobody lives there."

Snooky was hurt. "I do, Bernard."

"No, you don't. Nobody lives there. You just visit from time to time."

"It's the end of January, Bernard. Have some pity."

"No. Please pass the syrup."

Bernard Woodruff was the antithesis of his wife and her younger brother. He was a big man, solidly built, with none of their pale, lean elegance. He had dark curly hair, a bristling beard, and soft, surprisingly amiable brown eyes. He looked like a different species altogether: like a brown bear mistakenly caged with a pair of whippets.

"Here's the syrup," said Maya.

"Thank you."

"I think you're making a mistake," Snooky said. "It's inhumanly cold up there. Inhumanly cold. You could go up there one day and find me frozen to death."

Bernard favored him with a pale glance. "I doubt it. I never go up there."

"I looked up the word 'inhuman' the other day. It means 'of or suggesting a nonhuman class of beings.' Is that what you consider me, Bernard—a nonhuman class of being?"

Bernard picked up the paper and began to read. Snooky sighed and dug morosely into his scrambled eggs.

Maya looked over at him affectionately. His real name was Arthur, but from infancy he had been nicknamed, for some obscure reason, Snooky. He had shown up at her house two weeks earlier, with a piece of battered luggage, a toothbrush in a brown paper bag and, he claimed, a heart recently broken in two by a siren from California named Deirdre Maxwell. They had been serious—quite serious, he said emphatically—when he came home one day to find that she had removed all her possessions from the apartment and left him for her medieval history professor at UCLA. The professor was a man in his late fifties with graying hair and, Snooky reported, a terrible paunch. Snooky was devastated; he had given up the apartment, boarded a plane to New York City, and appeared without warning on Maya's front step. One look at his face and she had taken him in without any questions.

Bernard, however, said he had a question.

"When is he going to leave?"

"Bernard," said Maya. "Please."

Bernard shrugged and turned away. He was used to Snooky's visits by now; they had occurred with a monotonous regularity ever since Snooky had turned twenty-one, come into his inheritance, and graduated from college. "A triple threat," his older brother William had said morosely at the time. "Rich, of legal age, and loosed upon the world to create havoc and destruction. We've created a monster, Maya. Do you understand what I'm saying? A monster of sloth and ingratitude."

William had raised the two of them after their parents had died in an accident. Maya was only twelve years old at the time and William, who was ten years older and well on his way to a successful career in corporate law, had taken care of them. In his considered opinion, Maya had turned out well: she had a job writing on various science topics for a small magazine called *The Animal World*, she was married and hardworking and respectable, she spent her money on sensible investments like a house. Snooky, on the other hand, was, in his older brother's eyes at least, a menace to freedom-loving individuals everywhere. He did not believe in working for a living, and he did not seem to want to settle in any one place. He thanked William politely for his part of the inheritance and then took off, traveling around the country, living here and there, depending on his whims. William felt as if he had inadvertently, due to some unlucky stroke of fate, raised the Antichrist to maturity. He spoke about Snooky as if he were dead.

"He was such a nice little kid," he would say reminiscently, tears in his eyes, "such a nice little kid. So *good*, Maya. So hardworking."

"I hate to break this to you, William, but Snooky was never hardworking."

"At least . . . at least he pretended, Maya. Do you know what I'm saying? At least he made an effort."

After his final exams and college graduation, it was difficult to discern what effort, if any, Snooky made about anything at all. He roamed across the country at will, avoiding only the small area of southern California where William and his shrewish wife Emily lived. Occasionally, if he felt William was living too well or getting too happy, he would pay them a visit, always calling well ahead of time and announcing in advance when he would depart. This was in sharp contrast to his sudden and unexpected ports of call in the small town of Ridgewood, Connecticut. Ridgewood was a beautiful little town with a New England flavor to it; it had a quiet Main Street lined with shops, surrounded by miles of winding lanes with tree-shaded houses, rolling hills and large blue lakes. Maya and Bernard had renovated a sprawling Victorian house on a narrow lane bordered with willow trees. The house was white with blue trim, had three floors and an attic, and was comfortable and cosy, filled with plants and antiques. Snooky had claimed the little bedroom on the third floor in the back for his own. He used the room for his prolonged visits, and sometimes, as in this case, for emotional recuperation.

"When I'm done eating, I'm going to give Bella a call," he said now. "Find out what's up. She's never actually stood me up before."

"Okay," said Maya. "Where's the paper? I want to do

the puzzle. Hmmmm. Hey, Snookers. A Chinese domestic bovine. Four letters."

Snooky was staring vaguely out the window. "Zebu, Maya. Z-E-B-U."

"Good. How about ten across—an Estonian island. Seven letters."

"Hiiumaa. H-I-I-U-M-A-A."

"That fits. How about a trumpeter's cloak, Middle Ages? Six letters, starts with a T."

Snooky was still staring out the window, his thoughts elsewhere. "Tabard. Come on, Maya, you should know that. T-A-B-A-R-D."

"I hate this," said Bernard.

"It's a gift, Bernard," said his wife. "Fourteen down. Neat and tidy, five letters, blank A blank T blank."

"Natty," Snooky said dreamily. Bernard pushed his chair back with a loud squeak and left the room.

"Oh, don't go, Bernard," called Maya. "We'll stop if you want. Oh, well. Let's see here. How about an ancient Etrurian city, four letters?"

A little while later Snooky finished up his meal and went to the kitchen phone. He dialed rapidly. "Hello, this is Snooky Randolph calling. Is Bella there, please?"

Maya, still seated at the table, could hear the sound of a woman's high-pitched voice on the phone.

"I'm a friend of hers," Snooky said. "I was supposed to meet her in the city last night. Why? What's wrong?"

There was a pause. Snooky slumped suddenly against the doorjamb.

"I see . . . yes . . . yes . . . I'm sorry. I'm terribly sorry. Yes. I'll . . . I'll call again."

He hung up and turned to Maya, who was horrified to see his eyes filling with tears. His face was even paler than usual. He looked like a small animal that had just been hit.

"She's dead, Maya—dead! *Murdered on her way out the door!*"

She went up to him and put her arms around him.

"I'm sorry, Snookers," she said. "I'm so sorry!"

Two elderly women stood talking in the kitchen of the Whitaker mansion, a large Georgian redbrick house with white pillars.

"*Murdered*," said the first one. She was tall and thin with a wizened little face. She spoke with a certain melancholy satisfaction. "Murdered, here, in this very house. Never thought I'd live to see the day."

"Shut up, MacGregor," said her companion, without

heat. She was a short squat woman who formed what appeared to be a perfect cube: all hard angles and edges. She had white hair pulled back into a tight bun. She was drying the dishes as MacGregor was washing them.

MacGregor apparently did not have the slightest intention of shutting up. "Strangled," she went on with relish. "Who would've believed it?"

"Shut *up*, I'm telling you, MacGregor."

"Police everywhere, swarming all over the house like—like insects. I never thought I'd live to see the day."

"MacGregor, I'm telling you to shut up. Do you hear me? Don't you go shooting your mouth off to the police, either. You're just hoping for a chance to talk to them, even though you don't know a thing about it, aren't you? Now, close that rattling mouth of yours and go ahead with what you're supposed to be doing, which is the dishes. And for heaven's sake, stop splashing that water everywhere, you're getting me wet. And no more talk about my poor niece Bella. It's none of your business, you understand?"

"Yes, Miss Pinsky," MacGregor responded meekly. "Whoops! Watch that water!"

Detective Paul Janovy looked around him with a dissatisfied air. He was standing in the luxuriously furnished living room of the Whitaker mansion. Janovy was a tall, fair-haired man with a broad, rather coarse face and a normally cheerful disposition. At the present moment, however, he was unhappy. One of Ridgewood's leading citizens had been murdered and so far he had not the slightest clue as to who had done it.

He said, "Fish?"

His subordinate, Detective Martin Fish, materialized at his side. Janovy's eyes dwelt on him with approval.

Martin Fish was an excellent second-in-command, a careful and reliable detective who happened to have been cursed with a marked resemblance to his own name. He was tall and thin, with a long sad face, large bulging eyes and a round mouth habitually pursed in thought. He looked, thought Janovy with affection, exactly like a flounder. When he was thinking hard he would open and close his mouth as if flapping his vestigial gills.

Now he flapped his mouth several times before saying, in a querulous tone, "Sir?"

"Fish, let's go over it one more time."

Fish nodded and said: "Bella Whitaker was found by her son, Albert Whitaker, when he arrived home last night at approximately twelve-thirty A.M. The deceased was lying, fully dressed in black evening clothes, on the floor of the front hallway near the door. She had been strangled with a narrow cord which lay on the floor nearby. We did a complete search of the house. Nothing was missing except the deceased's left earring, which could not be found." Fish paused. He was much too fond of the word "deceased," thought Janovy in irritation. He would have to mention it to him.

"What did your men find? Had any of the doors or windows been tampered with?"

It was a cold night, replied Fish, and the windows were all locked from the inside. So was the back door. Albert Whitaker had stated that the front door was locked, as usual, when he came home. Fish's men confirmed that the lock had not been tampered with.

Janovy nodded. So the murderer, whoever it was, had a key to the house. Either that, or was well enough known by Mrs. Whitaker to be allowed in. "What did the medical examiner say?"

Fish consulted the report. "Death by strangulation,

between seven-thirty and nine o'clock P.M. No signs that the deceased put up much of a fight. She must have been taken by surprise."

I'll really have to talk to him about this "deceased" business, Janovy thought irritably. Aloud he said, "I imagine death by strangulation is nearly always a surprise. All right, Fish. Please tell Albert Whitaker I'd like to see him now."

Fish ushered in a big, hulking giant of a man, who crossed to where Janovy was standing, shook hands affably, looked around vaguely as if trying to figure out where he was, sat down on the opposite sofa, and knocked over a small brass table lamp. Albert Whitaker muttered, " 'Scuse me," righted the lamp, wiped his hands hastily on his trouser legs, ran a hand agitatedly through his thick fair hair, looked around, dropped his wire-rimmed glasses, and spent a minute or two fumbling for them on the sofa. Finally he put the glasses on with a certain dignity, sat up, and said, "Yes. How can I help you, Detective?"

Detective Janovy had watched all this with curiosity and interest. Naturally Albert Whitaker was his primary suspect—he had found the body, after all—and the man certainly had the strength necessary to strangle his mother. Not, Janovy reminded himself, that it would have taken much strength to overcome Bella Whitaker, who was, after all, nearly seventy years old. But now, upon first acquaintance, it seemed somewhat unlikely that Albert Whitaker would murder anyone. He didn't seem coordinated enough, for one thing. And there was a gentleness in his face that seemed at odds with the idea of violent death.

"Mr. Whitaker, please believe that we're very sorry to have to trouble you at such a time."

"Thank you," he said, again with that curious dignity.

"Would you please tell me where you were last night?"

"Certainly," said Albert Whitaker, and dropped his glasses again. He retrieved them quickly, muttered "*Damn!*", wiped them with a corner of his sweater, put them back on, stared in a startled, inquisitive fashion at Janovy as if he had never seen him before, then said matter-of-factly, "I was out for the evening with a good friend of mine."

Fish was ready with his notebook open and pen poised. Janovy said, "Your friend's name?"

"Gretchen. Gretchen Schneider. She lives at forty-three ninety-five Fungus Grove. No, excuse me, it's not Fungus, it's that other word . . . I always get the two confused. . . ."

"That's all right, Mr. Whitaker. We can look it up."

Albert Whitaker was peering worriedly out the window. The winter sunlight, pale and clear, flooded in and lit up his face. He was handsome in a rumpled, mussed-up way; even his face looked curiously disarranged, the nose a little too big, the mouth too wide, the eyes moonlike behind the lenses. It was a pleasant, sensitive face. He said, "No, not *fungus* . . . damn, what's that other word? . . . I always forget. . . ."

Janovy glanced at Fish.

"*Fruitcake* . . . no . . . I know, I have it, it's *Palomino*," Whitaker said at last in triumph. "Forty-three ninety-five Palomino Grove."

Janovy regarded him doubtfully. "You get 'Palomino' confused with 'Fungus'?"

Albert Whitaker gave him a sweet smile. "Yes . . . yes, stupid, isn't it? It has something to do with something I read

once . . . something about cowboys galloping across fields of mushrooms . . . somewhere out west . . . I can't remember now. . . ." He paused and squinted out the window again.

"Mr. Whitaker. Please go on. You were out with your friend—"

"Oh, yes. We had dinner at the Golden Eagle, you know, that restaurant in the center of town—"

Janovy nodded. Everyone in Ridgewood knew the Golden Eagle, famed for its hearty portions and low prices. "You went there straight from work?"

"Yes. We went together. I'm a professor of European history at Edgemont, the local college here, you know, and Gretch—Dr. Schneider, I mean—teaches English. We met after classes and went straight over to the Golden Eagle."

"What time did you arrive there?"

This took a bit of figuring out. The class was his last of the day, the one on Florence and the Italian Renaissance, and it was usually over . . . let's see now . . . around five-thirty, so that would mean he went over to the administration building to meet Gretch—he corrected himself, Dr. Schneider—around five forty-five, so they would have been at the restaurant by . . .

"Six-fifteen," said Janovy. Edgemont College, a small unpretentious place which gave an excellent education, was no more than half an hour's drive away, if that. "Thank you, Mr. Whitaker. Dr. Whitaker, I should say. And after dinner—?"

After dinner, around eight o'clock, they had walked over to the art gallery in the center of town, a little place called Happy Dreams. Thinking on this, Albert Whitaker became quite enthused. He ran his fingers through his hair, dropped several pencils from obscure pockets in his clothing, and unfastened his watch and fastened it on again.

"Fascinating show. Fascinating show of aboriginal art. The most amazing drawings I've ever seen. I would have loved to have bought some—in fact I'd have bought everything I saw, the whole show, except of course on a professor's salary I couldn't afford it. Still, Gretch and I are thinking of pitching in together—*oh!*"

He gazed, stricken, at the two detectives.

"Now you'll think I wanted the money. Damned stupid thing for me to say to the police, I guess. *Damn* it. Oh, well."

"How much money did your mother have, Dr. Whitaker?"

Janovy expected a startled stare and some obfuscations, perhaps some more pencils or pens dropping out of unexpected places, but instead Albert Whitaker merely nodded and came to the point with unexpected brevity.

"One hundred and twenty million dollars, Detective."

It was Janovy's turn to be stunned. One hundred and twenty million dollars! As luxurious as the Whitaker mansion was, he somehow had not expected them to be that rich. "Yes, well," he said, casting a glance at Fish, whose impassive face and bulging eyes revealed nothing. "Yes. And who stands to inherit the money?"

Albert Whitaker said calmly that there were just the two of them: himself and his sister Susan. "There's also my great-aunt Etta—she's around here somewhere today, probably in the kitchen—but I'm fairly sure Mother didn't leave her anything. My great-uncle left Etta very comfortably off."

Janovy nodded. "Please go on, Dr. Whitaker. How long were you at the art gallery?"

Albert Whitaker said he and his friend were at the gallery until it closed, at ten o'clock. Then they went over to the bar in town, The Painted Man, for a drink or two. He drove Gretchen to her house and got home himself around twelve-thirty. He went into the house—

"Was the door locked?" interrupted Janovy.

Albert paused. Yes, yes, the door was locked, just like always. He used his key to get in.

"Who else has a key to the house besides yourself, Dr. Whitaker?"

Albert Whitaker looked baffled. Just his mother and his sister, he said. No one else that he knew of. Oh, and Mrs. MacGregor, of course.

"She's our combination housekeeper and cook. She's been here for years. You'll find her in the kitchen if you want to ask her about it."

"Thank you, Dr. Whitaker. Please go on. You were out for the evening with your friend. . . ."

Oh, yes, said Albert Whitaker. It was a pattern, you

see . . . he and Gretchen always went out on Friday nights, had dinner, took in a show or a movie, then ended up the evening at The Painted Man. He usually got home at around twelve-thirty. Last night, as he was saying, he had opened the door just like always and gone in.

At this point in the narrative he stopped abruptly and turned a delicate shade of green.

"Thank you, Dr. Whitaker. You don't have to tell us any more. Just a few more questions, if you don't mind. Was anyone supposed to come by and see your mother last night? Anyone at all?"

"No, not that I know of. You see, my mother was going into New York City last night, so naturally she hadn't made any other plans."

"New York City," Janovy said thoughtfully. "Why? Was she meeting someone?"

"Yes, a young friend of hers. His name is Snooky Randolph. He comes in from time to time to stay with his sister, and always calls my mother to say hello, I must have his sister's address around here somewhere . . . let me think. . . ." He gazed around him doubtfully. "Now I wonder where I could have put it . . . ?"

"What's his sister's name?"

"It's an unusual name," Albert said helpfully. "Starts with an M, I think, or maybe an N. Sounds something like 'Aztec.' No, that's not right . . . hmmmm . . . let me see now. . . ."

It took several minutes of wild guesses and random word associations before Albert managed to dredge up the name. "Maya," he said triumphantly. "Maya Woodruff."

"Thank you. Do you know where your mother and her friend were planning to meet downtown?"

"No . . . no, I don't. All I know is she got all dressed up to go out. She was so excited about the date . . . she hadn't been to New York for such a long time. . . ." His voice trailed off.

"Yes," said Janovy briskly. "Once again, Dr. Whitaker, you're sure you don't know of anyone who might have come by here last night—perhaps just dropped by?"

"Oh. No, I don't. I was away all day, you see. You'll have to ask Mrs. MacGregor about that. She would have been here until around six or six-thirty, I guess."

"Fine. One last question, then. Was the money your mother's absolutely?"

Oh, yes, Albert said. His father had made a fortune in pins, and had left everything to his mother.

"Pins?"

"Pins. Straight pins, safety pins, diaper pins—until they went out of fashion—all kinds of pins."

"None of the money was left to you or your sister?"

Oh, no, Albert replied. His father had trusted his mother's judgment implicitly on everything, including the distribution of his wealth. And his mother had not so much distributed as doled out her money in dribbles.

"But it's not the way it seems," Albert said earnestly. He moved forward with an expansive gesture, and the brass lamp tottered on its base. "We're not murderers. You don't know us, that's all. You'll see when you meet my sister. It's not the way it looks."

I'll be the judge of that, thought Janovy. Aloud he said, "Thank you very much, Dr. Whitaker. You'll be hearing from us if we have any more questions."

Detective Janovy ran Mrs. MacGregor to earth in the big old drafty stone-walled kitchen. The room was cold and damp, and MacGregor was mopping the floor with a lugubrious expression. At the big wooden table in the middle of the room, someone who Janovy realized could only be Great-aunt Etta stood rolling dough around and around in her floury hands.

"Mrs. MacGregor?"

Mrs. MacGregor grudgingly stopped what she was doing and leaned on her mop. "Yes?"

"I wonder whether you would mind answering some questions about last night."

Mrs. MacGregor looked more sour than ever and said she didn't know. She cocked an unfriendly eye at him and said she didn't cotton to having police in the house, if he got her meaning.

Janovy said yes, he did, but if she could only answer a few questions—

MacGregor announced that it wasn't a matter of whether she *could* answer his questions; it was more a matter of whether she *would*, if he took her meaning.

Janovy said yes, but—

"Go ahead and talk to the man, MacGregor," said Etta Pinsky with sudden vigor. "You've been dying to talk to the police all day."

MacGregor was offended. That wasn't true. She was just doing her job—

"She's been talking about nothing else," Great-aunt Etta said dryly. "Go ahead, MacGregor. Here's your big chance."

Detective Janovy said that he was very interested in finding out who might have come into the house the previous evening—say, around seven-fifteen or perhaps later? Was Mrs. MacGregor in the house then?

MacGregor gave a loud sniff and said she was not, she was home by that hour, as every decent soul would be. She had left the house a little after six-thirty. Although now that he mentioned it . . .

"Yes?"

MacGregor cast a sly look at Etta Pinsky, who was busily rolling the dough back and forth. Well, she had been in the back of the house, MacGregor said. In the kitchen, where they were now. And just before she left, she had heard the front door open and close.

"What time would that be?"

MacGregor looked sour and said she didn't know. Around six-fifteen or six-twenty, maybe. Just before she left. But when she went out into the front hall to get her coat, there was no one there.

So the murderer came in earlier, thought Janovy. He or she came in and waited somewhere for Bella Whitaker to leave. "Did you leave by the front or the back door, Mrs. MacGregor?"

MacGregor looked upset and had to be calmed down before she would continue with the questioning. The back door, indeed! Who did he think he was, implying that she would sneak in and out the back door like—like a *servant*! Why, she had been here nearly ten years now. . . . She was like a member of the family. How *dare* he?

"I'm sorry," said Janovy hastily. "So you left, naturally, by the *front* door. Did you notice anything wrong with the door, or the lock?"

MacGregor pondered this and said no. Everything was as usual.

"Who else besides yourself has a key to the house?"

Just the family, said Mrs. MacGregor. Mrs. Whitaker and her two children.

"Did anyone come into the house yesterday afternoon or evening that you know of—anyone at all?"

MacGregor was firm on this topic. No one, she said. No one at all. She and Mrs. Whitaker were the only ones in the house, as far as she knew, and Mrs. Whitaker had spent most of the afternoon upstairs in her room.

"Would you be sure to hear if someone came in the front door—as you did around six-fifteen?"

MacGregor replied that she couldn't be sure exactly. If she was in the laundry room or working hard in the kitchen (at this point Great-aunt Etta gave a muffled snort), she might not hear. It was a long way from the kitchen to the front door. If she was washing dishes, for instance, she might not hear.

"One more question, Mrs. MacGregor. When you left, you locked the door from the outside?"

MacGregor gave him a particularly unfriendly look. "Of course I did. I always lock the door. What's the use of having a key otherwise?"

"Thank you very much, Mrs. MacGregor. You've been very helpful."

Janovy's interview with Etta Pinsky was short and very much to the point. She told him that she had been at home all last night. She lived in an apartment about fifteen minutes away. She was Bella's maternal aunt and in the sixty-eight years since Bella had been born they had gotten along just fine. She was, she informed him, seventy-nine years old, and would be eighty very soon. If he thought that at her age she was capable of jumping around and strangling people to death, particularly her well-loved niece, then he was, she said flatly, out of his mind.

Detective Janovy felt all at once that he was nine years old again and his favorite aunt had caught him in the process of systematically destroying his brother's toys. He barely had time to say a meek "Yes, ma'am," before Great-aunt Etta told him she had a loaf of bread to see to, and sent him packing.

He went out into the front hallway and stood looking thoughtfully around him. The hallway was big and square, with a spectacular grand staircase opposite the front door. There were archways on the other two sides of the square, one leading to the living room, the other to the dining room. Between the staircase and the archway to the living room was the front hall closet. Janovy crossed over to it and opened the door. The closet was small and narrow. It smelled faintly musty. He poked around between the coats. No room for anyone to hide in here.

The outlines of the murder were becoming a little clearer now. The murderer had come into the house around six-fifteen, hidden somewhere in or near this hallway, and waited until Bella Whitaker came sweeping down the red velvet carpet of the staircase. Then the murderer had come up behind her and killed her. Janovy looked around again. Where had that person hidden for over an hour?

Not in the closet, certainly. Either in the living room or the dining room, near the archways leading to the front hall. Either of them would allow the murderer to come up quickly and silently behind someone headed toward the door. Or . . .

Janovy walked around behind the staircase. There was a space there, between the stairs and the floor, a space just about the height of a man, a reasonably sized, dark hiding place. . . .

He stood behind the stairs for a long time, feeling his skin prickle. This was it, he was sure of it. This was where someone had stood last night and waited.

He walked around the staircase. If someone stood still

in the shadows, he or she could not easily be seen. Mrs. MacGregor, coming in from the dining room, must have passed right by the murderer on her way to the coat closet.

Shame, thought Janovy. It's a shame she didn't see anything. If she had only turned her head . . .

He went back into the kitchen and asked her about it. Mrs. MacGregor propped her elbow on her mop and replied in a nasty tone that she had told him all she knew. No, she hadn't seen anything or anyone in the hallway when she left. No, she hadn't looked at or under the stairs. She had better things to do with her time than go nosing about where it wasn't any of her business.

She said the last bit in a way that made it clear she thought that *he* should have better things to do as well. Janovy thanked her and left.

2

Bernard and Maya were standing over Snooky's bed watching him as he slept.

"He looks like a child when he's asleep," Maya said fondly. "Like a child."

"Everyone looks like a child when they're asleep, Maya. Don't get sentimental. He was in shock, you say?"

"Yes. All white and trembly. He *does* have feelings, you know, however rudimentary they may be."

Bernard looked thoughtfully down at the slumbering Snooky. "You gave him some brandy?"

"Yes."

"Not the good stuff, I hope?"

"Yes, Bernard. The good stuff. Let's go downstairs, shall we? I'm about to start screaming at you and that might wake him up."

They went down to the second floor and into Bernard's study. He sat down behind his massive desk and Maya perched on the edge of his chair. He put an arm comfortingly around her waist.

Mrs. Woolly

Bernard, like his wife, was a writer; he wrote children's books about mice, rats and sentient sheep. His
most popular creation so far was a maternal ewe with
eyeglasses and a gentle, kindly expression. Her name was
Mrs. Woolly. She was old and kind and long-winded, and
tended to get in and out of various difficulties.

Now Bernard took a page from his typewriter and
crumpled it in disgust. "Do the police have any idea who
did it?"

"Bernard, how would I know? Anyway, how could
they? It was just last night."

There was a silence. Maya put an arm around her
husband's shoulders and said miserably, "Murder, Bernard."

"Yes."

"Murder . . . and Snooky."

"Yes. Have you noticed how, whenever your brother comes to visit, the long arm of the law invariably follows?"

"Yes. I've noticed that." Maya absently fixed his collar.

Bernard looked at his wife's drawn, anxious face. "Have they considered suicide?" he asked gently.

"Suicide?" She gave a questioning look. "No. I don't know. Why should they?"

"I just thought the woman might have killed herself in order to get out of the date with Snooky."

"Bernard, I don't think I have to tell you that's not very funny."

"It's not out of the realm of possibility, though, is it? Wasn't there that woman who left the country rather than date him?"

"Bernard, please. She didn't leave the country. She had an emergency business meeting in Tokyo. They went out after she got back. Snooky still talks about her."

"How about this girl in California who packed up and left in the middle of the night?"

"It wasn't the middle of the night. Snooky was away, that was all. And she's an exception, you know that as well as I do. Snooky's usually very successful with women. He's very good-looking and there's something about him that makes women want to mother him."

"I know someone who likes to mother him," Bernard said sadly.

"Well, I'm not going to defend myself. He's my little brother and our mother died a long time ago."

Bernard had lost interest in Snooky. He was gazing out the window with a contemplative, faraway look in his eyes. "*Murder*," he said softly.

*   *   *

Ridgewood was a small town and, as in most communities large and small, news traveled rapidly. Bella Whitaker, while one of the town's leading citizens, a position she had enjoyed immensely right up until her untimely death, would have been dismayed to find that the general reaction was one of amused speculation on how much money she had had.

"Of course the children get it all," said Jessie Lowell, a plump faded woman in her forties who ran the local day-care center. "All that money!"

Her friend, Gretchen Schneider, smiled at her with affection. "I really do believe you're enjoying this, Jessie. It's a whole ghoulish side of you that I never knew about."

"Well, Gretch, of course a death is never *pleasant*, and I suppose I should feel terrible, but really, it's not as if I knew any of them except for Albert . . . I mean, I know them to say hello to because they live in town, and I've met Mrs. Whitaker once or twice—you remember, she donated some very nice pieces of pottery to the rummage sale last year . . . some nice pottery, and some old clothing that was still in wonderful shape, to tell you the truth, if it were mine I would *never* have given it away. . . ." She wandered on in this vein for a while. Jessie Lowell had a tendency to wander, although if recalled to the point she could think on one thing at a time quite lucidly.

"Well, I must say I feel terrible for Albert. He sounded so upset when he called this morning," Gretchen said finally in a firm tone, cutting through her friend's pleasant reminiscences concerning a fine alabaster vase that someone had given to the rummage sale.

"Oh, yes, poor Albert, poor poor Albert, it's so terrible for him. It gives me the shivers to think that I drove by there last night. I often take the long way home from work, because it's prettier, you know, and even though it was pitch dark I took it anyway last night, because I had some things on my mind and needed time to think. I'm having the worst time with some of my children, you can't imagine, of course I've told you all about Nathan, but yesterday Tiffany clamped on to one of the tables and wouldn't let go when her mother came to pick her up, I was afraid we'd have to sedate her or something awful like that—"

"You drove by the Whitaker house last night?"

"Why, yes, Gretch, I thought I told you. Oh, that's right, you were out too, weren't you? Well, I drove by and—"

"Did you see anything?" Gretchen asked sharply.

"Oh, no, no, of course I didn't. I mean, it was *dark*, really dark. The porch light was on, but it was all out of the corner of my eye, I couldn't see anything. Anyway, my mind was elsewhere, like I'm telling you. Tiffany is just getting worse and worse, and she's been so much on my mind lately, I'm really feeling quite worn out about it. . . ."

Jessie warbled on happily in this fashion for a while. Finally Gretchen said, "I suppose the police will be here soon."

Jessie paused and looked at her doubtfully. The police? Why? Why in the world would they come here?

"Well, you see, dear, I was out with Albert last night. We always go out on Fridays, you know. He told me this morning the police would be over to check on his whereabouts."

Jessie thought this was ridiculous. His whereabouts, indeed! Why, Albert Whitaker was such a *nice* man, such an intelligent and nice man, and now he was rich, too—oh, just think of it! Just *think* of it!

Gretchen looked at her friend's plump face, all red

with excitement, with its cheerful pug features and shining eyes. She felt a surge of affection. "You'd like all that money, wouldn't you, Jessie?"

"Well, of course," Jessie said eagerly. "Who wouldn't?"

"*I* wouldn't."

"Oh, come on now, Gretch. Don't be silly. Of course you would." Jessie looked at her friend reproachfully.

The two women were old college friends who had shared the same house since Jessie Lowell's divorce ten years earlier. Jessie was short, plump and expansive; her friend was tall, thin and confined. Gretchen had small pointed features and a sallow face. Her thin dark hair was cut short in a severe shingle. She moved jerkily and without grace.

"Oh, no I wouldn't. Money is a trap."

"Oh, that's just a truism. Money is freedom. You've never been divorced, you don't know what it's like to be suddenly left with nothing. Nothing! Why, I think Lenny would have been happy, positively *happy*, to see me starve on the streets. . . ."

She was off again. Gretchen sighed to herself. She usually enjoyed her friend's volubility, but not when it turned ugly, as it invariably did when Jessie discussed her ex-husband.

"Look at the time," she interrupted. "My goodness, it's late! What should we do for lunch today? It's so cold out and I don't feel like cooking. How about if we treat ourselves to lunch at the Golden Eagle?"

Jessie thought that was a wonderful idea. The Golden Eagle! Why, it had been *months* since she had been there. And perhaps they would hear more about the police investigation and the murder and everything . . . oh, yes, that was a *wonderful* idea!

*   *   *

Detective Janovy knocked on the door of the small house which was third from the corner on Maple Avenue. It was painted a robin's-egg blue with yellow shutters and looked, he thought, rather incongruous among its staid neighbors with their facades of white, cream, and gray. The door was opened by a small towheaded child of around four or five who gazed at him out of angelic blue-green eyes.

"Yeah?"

"Is your mother home?"

"Yeah." The boy turned, yelled *"MOM!"* in earsplitting tones, then shut the door in Janovy's face.

The door was opened a few minutes later by a young woman with a frazzled-looking expression. She was talking furiously, but not to Janovy. "Now, Harold, I've told you a million times, you can't just close the door on a visitor—Harold? . . . Harold, are you listening? . . . oh, that boy, I can't do a *thing* with—oh, hello," she said. "Can I help you?"

"Susan Whitaker?"

"Yes?"

"I'm Detective Janovy, of the Ridgewood police. May I come in?"

"Oh—oh, of course. Please. This way."

She led him into the living room, which Janovy noted was cramped but comfortable. The furniture looked a little worn (doubtless, thought Janovy, from the angelic Harold jumping up and down on it), and the floor was cluttered with toys and books and even what appeared to be articles of Harold's clothing (Janovy could see one shoe lying forlornly in the corner). The atmosphere was homey and comfortable. Susan Whitaker cleared a plastic train, a purple laser gun, and a miniature robot off one of the sofas and motioned for him to sit.

"He's been particularly difficult today," she said, settling in a chair. "Since we heard about my poor mother's death. It would be a shock anyway, of course, but he and my mother were very good friends."

"I'm sorry to have to disturb you now."

"That's all right. I understand you have a job to do."

Janovy sat looking at her in frank appreciation. Susan Whitaker was in her early thirties. She had a round, cheerful face, dark gray eyes, and curly red-gold hair drawn back and held in place with a rubber band. Her skin was pink and freckled and she exuded an air of exuberant well-being. She was slightly plump, and was wearing a rust-colored running suit. She grew slightly nervous under his gaze, and began to twist a tendril of curly hair round and round in her fingers.

Janovy said, "What do you do for a living, Miss Whitaker? I assume your name is still Whitaker, is that right?"

"Oh, yes. After the divorce, I took back my old name. I didn't want anything of my husband's, believe me."

"And where do you work?"

"I'm a journalist for the local paper—you know, the *Ridgewood Star*. I write a column on child care—some people who have met Harold think that I'm not really qualified to tell other parents how to raise their children—and I do a little reporting, whatever's around. Nothing too exciting. I'm afraid my mother's death will be the big news around here for a while."

"What was your relationship with her?"

"My mother? Oh, well, not too good, really. I mean, I left home years ago to get married—I was way too young, but I was desperate to get out. Then, after the divorce, I moved back here with Harold. I don't know why . . . I'm close to my brother and I guess I wanted to be near him. And Harold always adored his grandmother."

"You were desperate to get out of the house?"

"Yes, well . . . my mother was a marvelous person, you know, full of life and all that, but she was a little *domineering*, if you know what I mean. Look at poor Albert, he's nearly forty years old and he still lives at home. Why do you think that is? It's because my mother liked it that way."

"She liked it that way?"

"Oh, yes. My father died a long time ago, and I think my mother liked to pretend she was still married—to Albert. It's terrible, but there it is. She liked having a man around the house, she said so all the time. Albert's been seeing some woman he teaches with for years now—they go out together once a week like clockwork—really, it's sort of pathetic. Just sneaking around behind my mother's back. Albert's the firstborn and I think my mother would have had a fit if he decided to get married. And he's so nice, he never even realized he was being—well, being *used*." She fell into a reverie, still absently twisting a lock of golden hair. Then she came out of it with a start.

"Oh, well, I shouldn't be telling you all this, should I? After all, you're the *police*."

"What about your relationship with your mother, Miss Whitaker?"

"Me? We didn't get along too well, I'm afraid. Recently I've gotten engaged again—to someone Mother didn't approve of at all. Not that that makes any difference to me. She hated my first husband, too."

"Your fiancé's name?"

"George Drexler." She gave him the address.

"Please tell me about last night, Miss Whitaker."

She gave him a sudden sweet smile, and her features, more symmetrical and ordered than her brother's, suddenly looked like his. She had none of his vagueness, but they had the same intelligent dark gray eyes. "Oh, my. My *alibi*. Well, thank goodness I have one. You'll have to take my word for it that I didn't know ahead of time I'd need it. But I guess I pretty much have an alibi every night, since Dora comes over all the time. That's my friend, Dora Kelly. She lives at three-twelve Old York Road—you know, near the fire station. I called her last night and she came over with her baby around—oh, around seven o'clock, and stayed until a little after ten. Before that, Harold and I had dinner here together, and after Dora left I went to sleep. Harold goes to sleep much earlier, around eight-thirty."

Janovy jotted down the times and the address. "Thank you. So you weren't at your mother's house anytime yesterday evening?"

"Oh, *no*."

"Did your mother have any enemies that you know of?"

She looked at him wearily, and for the first time he could see the fatigue and sadness in her eyes. "No . . . not that I know of. My mother was very popular in this town, you know, Officer. A leading citizen and all that."

"Yes. One more question. Why didn't your mother approve of your fiancé?"

Susan shrugged impatiently.

"For the simple reason, Officer, that George is poor. My first husband was poor, and I had to ask my mother for some money to help tide me and Harold over the rough spots after the divorce. She had so much, of course, it shouldn't have mattered, but somehow it did. And then when she found out that George and I were thinking of getting married, she had a fit. She said she wouldn't support another poverty-stricken husband of mine. She said some pretty ugly things." She flushed. "It doesn't make any difference to me, of course. I've always done pretty much what I wanted. And Mother would have come around eventually."

Janovy sat looking at her thoughtfully. Susan Whitaker, he decided, was really a very attractive woman, all the more so because she seemed completely unconscious of her good looks. Now she gave a muttered exclamation, undid the rubber band binding her hair, and let it loose over her shoulders in abundant red-gold waves. Then she gathered it deftly up, twisted it into a bun and fastened it with a large tortoiseshell clip she scooped up from the floor.

"Harold plays with these things," she said by way of explanation. "I suppose I should worry about it, but then there are so many things about Harold I have to worry about. Which reminds me, he's so upset today that I really should be around in case he needs me. Is there anything more?"

No, said Janovy, and thanked her politely. She showed him to the door, made sure that he had both addresses down correctly, and waved him a friendly good-bye.

Dora Kelly turned out to be a buxom blonde with baby-doll features. She insisted on breastfeeding her infant daughter during the interview. Janovy found it difficult to focus his eyes anywhere in particular. Dora, however, was not perturbed by this. She laughed and said in her booming voice, "Don't know where to look, do you? Hah! Men! They're all the same!"

She detached the infant, whose name appeared to be

Pumpkin or Pooh, Janovy was not sure which, and said heartily, "Now, what's all this fuss? What are you running all around town for, stirring up people and asking them stupid questions? How do you know that Bella Whitaker didn't commit suicide, huh? Huh?"

Janovy replied cautiously that no one in his experience had ever succeeded in strangling themselves to death.

"Maybe there was a hook, and she hanged herself," Dora volunteered. The prospect did not seem to faze her. She attached Pumpkin to her other breast and boomed, "All right, then! Ask away! I did it! I'm the guilty one!"

Janovy's normally cheerful expression vanished and he proceeded with alacrity to take control of the interview. "How long have you known Susan Whitaker?"

"Susan? Why, we've been friends since we were in grade school together. Ever since I was a little girl. I lost touch with her when she got married and moved away, but we've been best friends ever since she came back here to live. That was about four years ago . . . that's right, four years ago. Harold was six months old. What a boy that is, eh, Detective? Did you get to meet him when you were there?"

"Did you go over to Miss Whitaker's house last night?"

"Yes, I did," Dora Kelly responded cheerfully. "We sat and had coffee and a nice long chat, let me think what it was about. Probably about Princess Di, you know, I'm *so* interested in anything to do with the Royal Family. Aren't you?"

Janovy glanced down at the stack of glossy magazines on the floor. Most of them featured photographs of the Princess of Wales on the cover. "No," he said frankly.

Dora laughed uproariously. "Ah, well, perhaps it's a woman's thing," she said. "A woman's thing. I suppose the psychologists would say it's a contrast with my own life, although to tell you the truth I'm perfectly happy here with Phil and the baby. I just like to read about the Royal Family. Makes sense, doesn't it?"

Janovy felt the interview slipping away from him again.

"Can you tell me the times you arrived and left Susan Whitaker's house?"

"Oh, my goodness, let me think—here, Pumpkin, I think that's enough for now, we might as well let the nice detective focus his eyes . . . that's right, there you go, little Pooh. What time I went over there? I guess it was around seven o'clock when I arrived. Yes, that's right, seven o'clock. I know because I had to leave in the middle of *Gilligan's Island*, right in the middle of the episode where the professor and Mary Ann—oh, well, you're not interested in that, are you? Anyway, I went over there around seven and left around ten o'clock. I know because Phil—that's my husband, Phil—was angry that I got home so late. He didn't like spending the evening alone. Oh, Pumpkin, what's *that*?"

That was a viscous gloppy white liquid which Pumpkin had suddenly thrown up all over her mother's lap. There was a short break in the interview while this was cleaned up. Three minutes later Dora sat back down with a hearty laugh and said, "Now, where was I?"

Janovy was feeling a little sick. He said, "Miss Whitaker told me that she's engaged."

"That's right." Dora Kelly glanced at him, and for an instant he got a view of a pair of disconcertingly shrewd blue eyes. Then the look was gone, to be replaced by her usual expression of near-idiotic vacancy. "To George. She told you about her mother's objections?"

"Yes. What more do you know about it, Mrs. Kelly?"

"Not much more. I know Susan's mother wasn't happy about the engagement, and I know Susan didn't care. But

George did. He cared a lot. He was all upset when Susan's mother threatened to cut her out of the will."

Janovy was interested in this. "Cut her out of the will?"

"That's right. She didn't tell you? Her mother pulled every string in the book. Susan said she didn't mean it, that she'd come around, but I don't know. She thought George was a loser and she didn't want him marrying her daughter."

"I see."

Dora said abruptly, "Well, Pooh, time for nappy-bye. Time for nappy-bye. How's that, little Pumpkin?"

Little Pumpkin seemed to think that was fine. She was cooing and making eyes at a nearby table lamp.

Dora Kelly looked at Janovy, and again he got a flash of intelligent blue eyes. "That'll be all, then?"

"Yes, Mrs. Kelly. Thank you for your time."

"You're welcome!" she boomed at him.

After the detective departed, Dora Kelly put her daughter down for a nap in her crib. She sang to her softly for a while, until Pooh (whose real name was Penelope) was sound asleep, splayed out in the effortless posture of babyhood. Dora went downstairs, made herself a cup of coffee, took out a big slice of crumb cake, and settled down by the phone.

She dialed rapidly. "Hello, Susie? It's me. He was just here—that detective, you know." She let out a booming laugh. "What a doll! I think—you know, I'm not sure, but I *think* you made quite an impression on him. That's right, Susan. Oh, don't laugh at me, your Auntie Dora knows about these things. That's right." She listened for a moment, then said, "Well, of course I did. Of course I did.

You know you can count on me, don't you?" Another booming laugh. "You can count on me!"

George Drexler met Detective Janovy at the door with an apron on and a large kitchen mitt shaped like a whale on his right hand.

"Excuse me a minute, just a minute, please come right in here," he said, ushering Janovy into the living room of his small apartment with a vague wave of the whale. He rushed back into the kitchen while Janovy glanced around. It was a pleasant little room with skylights and two big square windows. Over in the corner was a music stand, stacked precariously high with folios. There was an old broken-down stereo on the bookshelves, with two speakers standing on the floor. The furniture was old and comfortable-looking. Janovy sat down on the sofa, which groaned in protest. George Drexler shouted from the kitchen, as if in response, "I'm coming, don't worry, I'm coming!"

"Take your time, Mr. Drexler."

George finally appeared, his face flushed, and sank down in a chair. He had neglected to take off his whale mitt, and now gestured vaguely with it. "Cinnamon loaf," he said. "Damned tricky. What can I do for you, Detective?"

"You're Susan Whitaker's financé?"

George smiled triumphantly. "That's right. Have you met her yet? Am I a lucky man, or what? Isn't she gorgeous? Terrible news about her mother," he said hastily. "Just terrible."

"I take it you're not very unhappy over Mrs. Whitaker's death?"

"Well, Officer, I can't say I am. Bella never liked me . . . no, she never liked me. She thought I wasn't good enough for Susan. Of course, I'm not, but then, who would be?"

Janovy regarded him silently. George Drexler was a tall, thin, gentle-looking man with large dark eyes. He had droopy brown hair, a faintly puzzled expression and an ascetic-looking face. His clothes were wrinkled and his shirt looked as if it could use a washing. Now he smiled and said:

"Bella never really knew me. No, she never really knew me. She hated me simply because I wasn't rich, and wasn't ever likely to be rich. She thought I would just sponge off of Susan, which is ridiculous. She never really gave me a chance to prove myself."

"What is it you do for a living, Mr. Drexler?"

He gestured toward the music stand. "I'm a violist. I'm trying for a concert career, of course, or perhaps steady work with a quartet, but until then I play where I can, here and there, whenever I get a call. Of course it doesn't pay the bills, so I also work for the *Ridgewood Star*. I write a weekly music column and do a little bit of reporting. Perhaps you've seen my column?"

"No, I'm afraid not."

"Oh, well. Not many people have. I review concerts in the city, that kind of thing. I don't mind the work, and it was through the *Star* that I met Susan, so I'm grateful for that."

"Please tell me where you were last night."

George, like Susan, looked faintly amused. "My alibi, you mean? Well, fortunately I have one. I got a call earlier this week from a group I play with now and again, and we gave a performance last night at a community center near Springfield, Massachusetts—nice little place. Good acoustics. I would have enjoyed myself, except the first violinist—it's an octet, a double string quartet, you know—anyway,

the first violinist insists on playing everything much too fast, so we whipped through the Mendelssohn Octet at a breakneck pace. It's supposed to be half an hour, and we were done with it in twenty minutes. My head was spinning, I'll tell you. Would you like to hear a little bit of it?"

Janovy opened his mouth hastily to say no, but it was too late. George Drexler had leaped out of his chair, whipped off his whale mitt, and opened a viola case. He took out his instrument lovingly and tightened the bow. Then, with a flourish, he went into what he described as the middle of the first movement of the octet. "And it was *here*," he said, talking as he played, "that that asshole Fred decided it wouldn't be allegro moderato anymore—no, no, it would be presto all the way. Can you believe that?"

He whipped through a few more bars and then, with a sheepish glance at Janovy, put his viola away.

"I'm sorry. I love an audience. Susan always yells at me for that. There's nothing I like better than to play."

"I see. Very nice, Mr. Drexler. Now, can you tell me exactly when you arrived for the concert, and when you left?"

"Oh, yes. The concert started at eight o'clock. It ended around ten-fifteen, maybe ten-thirty. It was a long drive, so I wasn't back here until about midnight."

Janovy noted the times down carefully. "Thank you, Mr. Drexler. What's the name of the group you played with?"

George said the group was called Philo Harmonia, and gave him the names and addresses of the other members. Then he went into the kitchen and came out holding a plate of fresh-baked bread. "Some cinnamon loaf?" he asked brightly.

Janovy refused and departed hastily, leaving George munching cheerfully on a thick piece of bread spread liberally with jam and butter.

Gretchen and Jessie had returned from their lunch at the Golden Eagle, replete with gossip they had gleaned from the waitress and several other diners, and were sitting in the living room poring over the newspaper when the doorbell rang.

Gretchen said mildly, "I expect that's the police."

She went to the door and came back with Detective Janovy firmly in tow. "Jessie, dear," she said, "will you excuse us for a few minutes? I think we'd be more comfortable in here instead of the dining room."

"Oh, of course—of course, Gretch—pardon me, I'll just be a second—now, where did the weekend section go? . . . and where's that book I was going to—*aah!*" She pounced. "I'm off now. What a pleasure meeting you—you know," she added hastily, "you know, Albert is truly a very nice man, I'm sure he *couldn't* be involved with—oh!" She had caught Gretchen's eye. "Well, I'll just be on my way now . . . good-bye!" She bustled away, her arms filled with books and papers.

Gretchen laughed quietly. "She's a dear person. All she lives for is to see me married. She has great hopes for me and Albert."

Janovy settled down in a big overstuffed chair by the fireplace and cast an approving glance around. The house was cramped, but neat and tidy; it was cosily furnished and some very beautiful watercolors hung on the walls. Gretchen followed his gaze.

"Jessie did those. She's very good, isn't she? I particularly like this one." She indicated a harbor scene with boats and sailing sloops. "That's from a few years ago, when we went down to Mystic for a few days. We stayed right on the water. I swam and Jessie painted." She moved across the room with her characteristic abrupt, graceless walk and folded herself stiffly into a chair. "But I don't think you came here to talk about our summer vacations, did you?"

"No, Dr. Schneider. I'm afraid not. Can you tell me where you were last night?"

Gretchen's account matched exactly with Albert Whitaker's. They had left the campus around five forty-five, arrived at the Golden Eagle a little after six, left there for the art gallery at eight and gone to The Painted Man when the gallery closed at ten o'clock. She had gotten home a little after midnight.

"It's our Friday night routine," she said dryly.

"You and Dr. Whitaker have been seeing each other for a while?"

A faint spark of some kind of emotion leaped in her eyes. "Nine years."

"And are you engaged?"

"No, we're not."

Janovy waited, but she did not seem disposed to go on. Finally she said with a little shrug, "Well, I don't really think Albert's the marrying kind. He's a confirmed bachelor. You know the type."

She seemed to be surveying him critically, as if he too were the type. He said, "What was your relationship with his mother?"

"Bella? It was civil, but that's all. She never took to any of his friends, and she certainly didn't take to me."

"And Dr. Whitaker's feelings toward his mother?"

"Oh, he was always devoted to her. Devoted. I think she pushed him around entirely too much, but Albert never even seemed to notice it."

"So you were with Dr. Whitaker all evening, then?"

"Yes."

"Tell me, did you tend to stay near him at the art gallery, or were the two of you walking around separately?"

"Oh, we were together." A faint smile crossed her face. "Albert lives at least ten or fifteen minutes away from the gallery, Detective. I'm quite sure I'd have noticed if he had left for nearly half an hour. No, I was at his side the entire time. A fascinating show—did he tell you? Aboriginal drawings. We're thinking of scraping together some money to buy some of them."

It wouldn't need much scraping, out of sixty million dollars, to find the necessary funds, thought Janovy. "I see. And that's your story, Dr. Schneider?"

She looked at him in an irritable way. "That's the truth, Detective."

"Thank you very much."

He rose to go, but Gretchen waved him back into his seat. "There's something else you should know, Detective. Jessie drove by the Whitaker place last night. She says she didn't see anything, but I thought perhaps she should talk to you anyway."

"Yes. Thank you. Would you please ask her to come in?"

Gretchen went out into the hallway and came back in a few moments with Jessie, who had a pencil stuck behind her ear, the weekend section in her hand, and a frightened look on her face.

Janovy said, "I understand that you were at the Whitaker house last night, Miss Lowell? What time was that?"

"Oh, no, no, no," she hastened to correct him. "I wasn't there, actually *there*—I mean, I just drove by in my car. I often take the long way around on my way home from work, and last night I had a lot of things on my mind, especially one little girl who's turning out to be a real problem. I don't think she likes her mother very much. I haven't decided what, if anything, to do about it—"

"Jessie," said Gretchen.

"Oh, yes. Yes, I'm sorry, Gretch. I drove by there last night. But it was dark, you know. Pitch black. I didn't *see* anything."

"What time was that?"

"Oh, let's see, it must have been a little after six or so. I usually leave work at five-thirty, but last night I was late because everything takes longer to tidy up at the end of the week, doesn't it? So I left around six, I guess. Not that I look at the clock very much. The one at the center runs fast and so I don't trust it. I have to remember to use my watch instead. I just got a new watch for my birthday and it keeps time beautifully. You see, it's gold and silver with a blue dial, I think it's quite striking—"

"When you went by the Whitakers', was the porch light on?"

Jessie contemplated this. "Was the porch light on? Yes, you know, I think it was. Oh, I'm sure it was. I only caught a glimpse of it out of the corner of my eye, of course."

"Was anyone parked in the driveway out front?"

Jessie said she didn't know. She wasn't sure. She was sure she didn't know. "It was *dark,* you see. It gets dark at five o'clock these days, doesn't it? I don't think I saw a car. Of course the Whitakers have that lovely sweeping driveway out front, but I don't think I saw anything. I wasn't looking, you see. I was thinking about little Tiffany, and all the trouble she's caused, and whether I should call in the child psychologist, I know a very good one, because I think she's really very *unhappy—*"

"Did you see anyone entering the house?"

Jessie replied firmly that she hadn't. She hadn't seen *anything.* She had just swooshed by in her car and glimpsed the house out of the corner of her eye. That was all.

Throughout this interview, Gretchen had been sitting primly in the corner, her hands folded on her lap. Now Jessie cast her an appealing look.

"Is that all, then, Gretch? Because I'm halfway through the paper, and I *did* want to finish before dinnertime."

"Yes, thanks, Jessie, that's all. Isn't it, Detective?"

Janovy got to his feet. "Yes, thank you very much. If you remember anything else, either of you, please give me a call."

"Oh, we will," said Gretchen. "We will."

Janovy sat in his car outside the house for a while. He grew steadily colder as the frigid winter air seeped in. He didn't like the way the interview had gone. He had the vague feeling that it had been stage-managed by Gretchen Schneider, and the thought made him very uneasy. Was there something he had missed? Something else he could have asked?

At any rate, Jessie Lowell, whether she realized it or not, had implicated herself. By her own admission, she had been at the scene at just about the time when the murderer had entered the Whitaker house. Who was to say that she had not stopped there herself, gone in, and put the rope around Bella Whitaker's neck?

Janovy sat there for a long time, feeling the early winter darkness close in on him. Finally he started the car and drove away.

Snooky woke up with a start, from a confused sleep filled with evil dreams and the disembodied heads of people he had known since childhood. Something large, dark and ominous was bending over him. He stared upward, terrified, and screamed at the top of his lungs.

The lights were switched on. Bernard said irritably, "Snooky, what in the world is the matter with you?"

"Oh. It's you, Bernard. I'm sorry." Snooky sank back onto the pillows. "I must have been having a nightmare or something."

"There's a detective downstairs who's asking to see you."

Snooky became aware that his head was throbbing mercilessly and the fact that he had screamed so loudly had not helped. "What time is it?" he whispered.

"Five-thirty. Nearly dinnertime."

"It's five-thirty in the afternoon and I have a hangover?"

"Maya gave you some of our best brandy before you took your little nap."

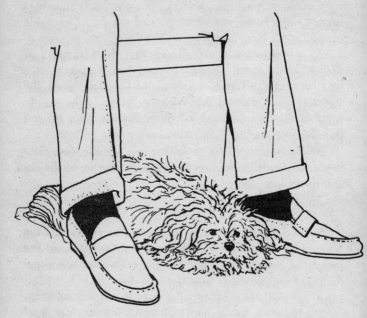

"Oh . . . right. Listen, keep the detective busy for a few minutes, will you? I'll be right down."

When Snooky came downstairs five minutes later, he found Detective Janovy and Bernard sitting on opposite sides of the living room, staring silently at each other. Misty, a small red fur ball of a dog, was sitting at Bernard's feet, also staring in a hostile way at the detective.

"Hello. I'm Snooky Randolph."

"Detective Janovy." They shook hands.

Bernard rose silently to his feet and moved off in the general direction of the kitchen.

"Brilliant conversationalist, isn't he?" said Snooky cheerfully. "Keeps us entertained for hours. How can I help you, Detective?"

"If you'll just answer a few questions about last night. . . ."

Snooky recounted in full his evening at Le Roi Soleil. He and Bella Whitaker were old friends; they had met years ago, when he was still in college, at a party in New York City. Whenever he came to town to visit his sister, he tried to give Bella a call. "I know the rest of the family, too," he said. "Albert and Susan. And Great-aunt Etta's a particular favorite of mine."

"You arranged to meet Mrs. Whitaker downtown?"

"Yes," said Snooky. He was going to be in New York during the day, so they had arranged to meet at Le Roi Soleil at eight-thirty.

"Mrs. Whitaker was killed, as you know, on her way out of the house. The earliest she could have been leaving was seven-thirty. It was a two-hour trip by train, so the earliest she could have been at the restaurant was nine-thirty. Was she usually that late?"

Snooky pondered this. "No, not really. Ten minutes, fifteen minutes, maybe, but not a whole hour. She must have been detained somehow."

"Yes. When did you set up this meeting with her?"

"Last Tuesday, on the phone."

"Did she mention to you having to see anyone before she left for New York?"

"Oh, no. She sounded great, said she was looking forward to seeing me. Everything sounded perfectly normal. I think if she had known somebody would be coming by on Friday she would have mentioned it to me. You know, I've been thinking about it, Detective, and I'm quite sure she didn't have the slightest idea that someone was planning to kill her."

Yes, thought Janovy. From what he had seen and heard so far, he thought that was absolutely true.

In the kitchen, a big country-style room with plants along the windowsill and copper pots hanging from the ceiling, Maya was chopping vegetables and Bernard had been set to tending the soup. He stirred and she chopped in silence. At last he said mournfully:

"The law, Maya."

"Yes, sweetheart."

"You can go for years without policemen showing up at your door, and then all at once, one day, there they are."

"Yes, sweetheart."

"Upsetting, isn't it?"

"Yes. How's the soup?"

"Under control."

"Good."

Silence.

"How's the new book going?" asked Maya.

"Not very well."

"What's the matter?"

"I don't know. I'm having a little trouble concentrating."

Bernard's book featured his newest creation, a large dandified white rat named Mr. Whiskers. So far Mr. Whiskers had spent most of his time pirouetting rather foolishly in front of the mirror, instead of getting into exciting scrapes.

Bernard pulled at his beard and frowned. "The damned creature seems to be a narcissist. I can't get him away from the mirror."

"Really? What a shame. Do you think there's anything Freudian about that, darling? Do you think you're a narcissist?"

"No," said Bernard. "I'm an anthropophobe. I'm not in love with myself, I just hate other people."

"Oh."

Silence.

"Listen to me, sweetheart," Maya said a little while later. She was chopping tomatoes into a pan. "I don't want you involved in this business with Snooky."

"I don't intend to get involved."

"I know you, Bernard. You're thinking about it instead of your work, and you're going to get yourself all upset over nothing."

"I will not," Bernard said with dignity. "I couldn't care less if all of Snooky's friends get it into their heads to kill each other off simultaneously. Maybe he'll come visit us less if everyone he knows around here is dead. What do you think?"

"I think you should drop it."

"Okay."

"You've got enough on your mind with Mr. Whiskers, don't you?"

"Mr. Whiskers can go to hell."

Maya raised an eyebrow. "That bad, huh?"

"Never write about rodents, Maya. Remember that. Never write about rodents."

"Thank you, sweetheart. I'll try to keep that in mind."

The funeral was held on a bright, clear, sunny day. Most of the residents of Ridgewood came to the church service. Mrs. Whitaker had been a favored citizen of the town; most people knew of her if they did not actually know her personally. There was a long, seemingly interminable sermon, the organist played a sad hymn, and everyone wept. Jessie enjoyed herself thoroughly.

"So *nice* to have a good long cry," she said, burying her face in the folds of a huge white handkerchief. "So *nice* . . . don't you agree, Gretch?"

"Hush, dear."

Afterwards the family and a small group of friends went out to the cemetery to see Bella Whitaker laid to rest, then back to the house for a quiet reception. Great-aunt Etta smiled grimly as Snooky came up to her and kissed one wrinkled cheek.

"So you're back in town for a while, are you, boy? Don't approve of the way you flit around from place to place. Unhealthy, that's what it is. You should stay in one place, marry and settle down. You can afford that, can't you?"

"Pardon me, Aunt Etta. For a moment I thought my older brother William was in the room. Strange acoustics in here."

"Oh, well, the young never listen to the old," she said philosophically. "No, no, they never listen."

Susan Whitaker came up and gave Snooky a kiss. Her eyes were swollen and red, but she still managed to glow with a kind of animal cheerfulness and vitality. She was dressed in black velvet, with a simple strand of pearls. Her hair was twisted back into an elaborate knot at the nape of her neck. "Snooky, how wonderful to see you. Even at this awful time. Has Aunt Etta been picking on you?"

"The old always pick on the young," grated Aunt Etta. "It's their only interest in life."

"I want you to come and say hello to Albert," Susan said, taking Snooky's arm. As she pulled him through the crowd, the musicians in the corner began picking their way with obvious trepidation through the Dvorak Piano Quintet. George Drexler, the leader, was playing with intense concentration and beating time in the air with his viola. Occasionally he could be heard saying in a loud, hoarse whisper, "Bar sixty-four! Bar sixty-four!" as one member or another of his little group lost their place. His large mournful eyes were half closed in ecstasy.

"Just look at him," Susan said with loving exasperation. "You haven't met George yet, have you, Snooky? The man lives for his music. I've never seen anything like it. I asked him to bring some friends and play for the reception, and he has to go and pick something none of them has ever tried before. The only saving grace, thank God, is that nobody is listening. Albert, say hello, will you?"

Albert was standing with Gretchen by the buffet table. He was looking pale and distraught. Snooky shook his hand and said, "Albert, I'm so sorry. Really. Sorrier than I can say."

"Thank you, Snooky. Have you met my friend Gretchen?"

As Snooky and Gretchen shook hands, George could

be heard saying in a loud whisper, "Bar ninety-three! Bar ninety-three!"

Meanwhile, Great-aunt Etta had not been idle. She had taken a firm grip on Bernard's arm, effectively preventing him from bolting, and was now saying in an aggrieved tone,

"Don't like it one bit. Not one bit. I don't like having strangers all over this place—why, it's like my own house. No, I don't like it."

"I can understand that," said Bernard with feeling. There was not much in this world that he disliked more than having a horde of strangers descend upon his house.

"You can, eh? You can? That's interesting. That's extremely interesting," she said in a tone which implied that it most definitely was not. "What did you say your name was again?"

Bernard repeated his name and found his hand crushed in a strong manlike grip.

"I like you," she said with a wintry smile. "I like the cut of your gib, if you know what I mean."

"I'm flattered," said Bernard.

"Although I don't suppose you youngsters use expressions like that anymore, do you? No, no. It's only old folk like me who still talk that way."

She leered up at him in a strangely provocative manner.

"You remind me of my husband," she announced. "That's why I've taken to you. That's why it is. My poor husband Vinnie. He's been dead, oh, more than ten years now. Would you like to know how he died?"

Bernard replied without hesitation that he would love to know.

"His head was crushed underneath a tractor," she said, with what seemed to be an undue amount of triumph. She let out a cackle. "Crushed underneath a tractor."

Bernard asked how such a bizarre accident might have taken place, and Etta expounded at length. "We were traveling, you know, in farm country in the south of France, and we were being shown around a working farm on a kind of tour, and Vinnie, who *always* had to stick his nose into everything, got down on his hands and knees while we were all away in the house and . . ."

The afternoon passed quickly. After a few hours the reception began to empty out. Bernard, his head spinning with details of Vinnie's unfortunate accident, plus details of Etta and Vinnie's travels all over the world in the happy early years of their marriage, was released from Etta's viselike grip with a stern admonition to come back sometime and see her soon.

"I like you, young man, and that's saying a lot," she said with icy satisfaction. "That's saying a lot."

Bernard liked her too, although he reflected that he could begin to understand why the luckless Vinnie, after thirty-five years of marriage, had gone and stuck his head under a tractor. Great-aunt Etta was a good talker. Anyone married to her would not lead a peaceful life.

On the way home in the car, Maya looked at him with a smile. "Quite the debonair man-about-town, aren't you, Bernard? Picking up eighty-year-old women at their relatives' funerals?"

"Wait, Maya. Wait till you hear this. I have an extremely touching story to tell you."

Dora and Phil Kelly, with Pumpkin in tow, arrived home after the funeral reception to find Detective Janovy waiting patiently on their front step. Dora let out an earsplitting shriek.

"It's the police, Phil—run for your life! Quick, take the

baby and make a break for it! You reach the trees and I'll delay him here!"

Detective Janovy remarked that he didn't think that was very funny.

"It's not, doll-face, you're right," Dora said, unlocking the door and motioning him inside. "What can we do for you today?"

Janovy said he'd like to have a few words with Mr. Kelly. Dora let out another shriek. "All right, doll-face, but don't work him over too hard, okay? Phil is a sucker for torture, he won't last a minute, will you, Phil? And Phil, you remember that story I told you to tell him, okay?—about where I was the night Mrs. Whitaker was killed?"

Janovy decided that he really did *not* like Dora Kelly.

"Pumpkin and I will be in the next room," she said, waving them into the living room. "You know what I'm saying, Phil. We'll be listening in on those wiretaps I just had installed."

Janovy sat down and took a good look at Dora Kelly's husband. Phil Kelly was a big muscle-bound guy with short blond hair and handsome clean-cut looks. He was wearing a suit and tie, but now he took off his jacket with a sigh of relief. He rolled up his shirtsleeves and said politely, "Yessir?"

"Mr. Kelly, could you please tell me where your wife was last Friday night?"

"She was over at Susie Whitaker's."

"Are you sure of that?"

Phil Kelly shrugged. "Course I'm sure. Where else would she be? Those two women are together all the time, yacking, yacking, yacking. Can't get a word in edgewise. Yeah, she took Pooh and the two of them went over there for a couple of hours. I remember because she was so late getting back."

"Can you tell me what time she left here and returned?"

"No problem." Phil rummaged around in a big pile of newspapers and came up with a *TV Guide*. "Last Friday, right? Let me see. Yeah, that's right. She left in the middle of *Gilligan's Island* and came back at the beginning of *Wheel of Fortune*. That would make it six forty-five to a little after ten. I tell you, those two girls can talk your ear off. Never seen anything like it."

Janovy gave up. "Thank you very much, Mr. Kelly."

"No problem."

As he left, Dora Kelly came to the door. "So long, doll-face. Did you get what you wanted? Did you have to pull his toenails out? Oh, Phil, you big slob, you told him everything, didn't you? Bye-bye now! Pumpkin, wave bye-bye to the nice policeman!"

3

"All right, Fish, let's have it," said Detective Janovy.

The two of them were sitting in his small cramped office. Fish closed his eyes, propped his chin against his steepled fingers as if praying, and said, "I talked to the waiters and waitresses at the Golden Eagle. Three of them remember seeing Albert Whitaker and Gretchen Schneider there last Friday night. They said the two of them are regulars there. Of course, who isn't?"

Janovy nodded. Everyone in Ridgewood was a regular at the Golden Eagle.

"The guard at the art gallery, Happy Dreams, doesn't know the two of them and didn't recognize them when I showed him photographs, but he's new in town and that doesn't mean much. He said the gallery was overflowing on Friday night because of the opening of the show, and there were too many people for him to remember. The bartender at The Painted Man said the two of them come in every Friday night for a drink. As far as he remembers, last weekend was no exception."

Janovy nodded. It didn't matter about the bar, anyway;

the critical times were seven-thirty to nine o'clock. "In other words, Whitaker's story checks out; but except for Dr. Schneider's word, he has no real alibi for the time his mother was killed, when they say they were at the art gallery."

"No, sir. No alibi." Fish coughed delicately. "And neither does she."

"That's right. What else, Fish?"

"Susan Whitaker placed a call to her friend Dora Kelly's house at six-thirty that evening. The call lasted three minutes. She could have been inviting her over, or—"

"Or not."

"Yes, sir."

"No way of knowing."

"No, sir."

Fish waited respectfully while Jonovy pondered this.

"What else, Fish?"

"Susan Whitaker's financé, George Drexler, wasn't in town that evening. He was at a community center near Springfield, just as he said. I spoke to the other members of Philo Harmonia, as well as some people who were in the audience that night, and they confirmed that he was there on time and played the entire performance."

"How far away is that?"

"About an hour and a half. No less."

"So he was away during the critical time?"

"Yes, sir."

"All right. What else do you have?"

"Etta Pinsky doesn't have an alibi. She says she was home that evening, but there's no one to confirm that."

"Think she could be in on it, Fish?"

Fish opened and closed his mouth silently as he thought. "I doubt it, sir. Where's her motive? Mrs. Whitaker didn't leave her any money. And why would she suddenly decide to kill her niece?"

"I agree. The will was read yesterday?"

"Yes, sir. Everything just as Albert Whitaker told us. The money was split evenly between himself and his sister."

"Sixty million each?"

"Sixty-four million."

Janovy leaned back and shook his head. Sixty-four million dollars! "I'd say the motive's pretty clear, then. What's the report on the fingerprints, Fish?"

Fish shuffled through some notes. "The only fingerprints on the front door were those of Mrs. Whitaker, Albert Whitaker, and Mrs. MacGregor."

"And in the hallway? Under the stairs?"

"In the hallway, just those three again. Under the staircase, none."

"Which is what you'd expect if the killer wore gloves."

"Yes, sir."

"What about the missing earring, Fish? Any idea where it went?"

"No, sir."

Janovy regarded him thoughtfully. "Why would the murderer take it? It doesn't make any sense. It's incriminating evidence."

"I don't know, sir."

"There's no sign of it anywhere—in her room, on the stairs, in the hallway?"

Fish shook his head in a melancholy fashion. Janovy sighed. "All right. Did you check up on who has a key to the house, Fish?"

"Yes. It was just as Albert Whitaker said. Mrs. Whitaker, her two children, and Mrs. MacGregor. Mrs. Whitaker's keys were in the evening bag she was carrying when she was killed. The other three showed me their keys, so none of them is missing."

"I see. That's interesting. One more thing, Fish. Mrs.

MacGregor says she heard somebody coming in around six-fifteen. But Bella Whitaker wasn't killed until seven-thirty at the earliest—even though she should have left for New York City by then. Speculation?"

"Someone she knew, sir. Someone who kept her talking for a while."

"Yes. I agree."

"Do you think it's possible, sir," Fish asked diffidently, "that this murder—well, that it wasn't planned in advance?"

"Not planned?"

"Yes, sir. I've been thinking . . . perhaps someone made an appointment with Mrs. Whitaker that evening. She agrees to see this person before she catches her train. The person comes by and they get into an argument. The visitor pretends to leave, but instead hides behind the staircase. When Mrs. Whitaker comes downstairs and heads toward the door, the visitor comes up behind her and kills her."

"A sudden impulse after the argument?"

"Well, something like that, sir."

Janovy sat thinking. It was possible . . . there was nothing to say that this was a well-planned murder. Just an intuition he had, that this was no hastily executed, ramshackle affair. . . .

"What would the argument be about, then, Fish?"

"I'm not sure, sir."

A sudden vision flashed in front of Janovy's eyes—bright red-gold hair, a glowing face, and intelligent gray eyes on his, while a voice said, . . . *when she found out that George and I were thinking of getting married, she had a fit . . . she said some pretty ugly things. . . .*

"Thank you very much, Fish," he said abruptly. "That'll be all."

"Yes, sir."

*   *   *

Mrs. MacGregor grumbled to herself as she got the broom out of the closet. Etta Pinsky said, "What is it, MacGregor?"

MacGregor replied in a surly tone that it was nothing, just her lumbago that acted up every now and again. Etta snorted and said that the only time MacGregor's lumbago acted up was when she was working. MacGregor bristled and had to be pacified before consenting to sweep the kitchen floor.

She was cleaning Etta's little apartment, something she did once a week. Etta watched her sharply. "You've missed that corner there, MacGregor. Good Lord! I have to keep my eye on you all the time."

MacGregor looked sour and said that wasn't true.

"Yes, it is, MacGregor. Look over there, you've missed that spot, too. Honestly, you're impossible."

MacGregor rested her elbow on top of the broom and remarked that her other clients didn't give her any trouble the way Miss Pinsky did.

"Other clients, indeed! Who exactly are you talking about?"

It turned out that MacGregor cleaned and cooked a bit for a few other households in town. There were the Whitakers, of course; there was old Mrs. O'Donnell who lived on that road with the name of one of those spices, MacGregor could never remember, parsley or cloves or oregano or something; there were Miss Lowell and Dr. Schneider over on Palomino Grove, and finally there were Mr. and Mrs. Milhausen on Russell Lane. Etta did not think much of this. "It's not my fault, MacGregor, if you persecute other people, too. And the name of that road is Nutmeg Lane. By the way, did you know that the Milhausens' son was getting married? Yes? To someone he met in the Peace Corps in Belize? Yes? Did Mrs. Milhausen say anything about it to you?"

The talk turned to topics of mutual interest and amused speculation.

"Letter for you," said Maya. "From California."

Snooky groaned. "Another from William?"

"I don't think so. The return address says Maxwell."

"Deirdre?" Snooky grabbed the letter and tore it out of the envelope. He scanned it rapidly.

Dear Snooky (it read),
I just wanted to let you know that Fred and I will be getting married this spring, and how sorry I am to have hurt your feelings. I am really, truly, deeply sorry that Fred and I met while I was living with you, and I wanted to make sure there were no bad feelings, because I have enough negative karma to worry about without adding this on. Please come visit us if you are ever back in this area. Yours in the Dharma, Deirdre

Maya scanned the letter, then put it down on the table. "Fred is the medieval history professor?"

"Yes."

"She sounds sensitive, Snooks. Really sensitive. One of your better choices. The part about the negative karma brought tears to my eyes."

"I'm going to scream," Snooky said despondently. "Excuse me, Maya. I'm going to go upstairs and scream."

"I wouldn't do that if I were you. Bernard's in his study, and you know how he is about loud noises."

"All right. I'll go into the living room and scream. I've never felt this bad in my entire life. Excuse me."

A little while later Bernard came downstairs and poured

himself a cup of coffee. He cocked his head toward the living room and said, "What's that thin wailing sound, Maya?"

"It's Snooky screaming."

"Really? Why is he doing that?"

"His girlfriend just wrote to tell him she's getting married."

Bernard read the letter, then checked his watch. "Do you think he'll be done soon? There's a program I want to watch at eight o'clock."

"I don't know, sweetheart. You could go ask him yourself."

"Never mind. I can watch upstairs on the little TV."

"You could get him to move if you wanted."

"No. It's good for him. Get his feelings out and all that."

"Very liberated of you, Bernard."

Bernard motioned toward the letter. "This girl doesn't seem to be much of a prize, does she?"

"No, but then, you know I never think anybody's good enough for him."

"Do you think you could maybe get him to tune down the high frequencies? Misty's upstairs in my study, and her hair's all standing on end."

"I don't know. I'll do what I can."

"Thanks."

"I've made a decision," Snooky said.

Maya passed him the bowl of mashed potatoes. "What's that, Snooks?"

"I've decided that I'm doomed never to have a success-ful relationship with a woman. Don't you agree, Bernard?"

"Yes."

"Therefore, I've decided to get a pet. You know. Like animal therapy. Someone to share my life with."

"Sounds pathetic," said Maya. "Any particular kind of pet in mind? Lions or tigers or bears?"

"Snakes," said Bernard, "are supposed to be extremely affectionate creatures."

"I don't want a snake."

Bernard heaped a mountain of mashed potatoes next to his teepee of green beans. "Tarantulas," he said mildly, "have very giving natures."

"I don't want a tarantula, thank you, Bernard."

"Why not? It would be so easy to pack up with the rest of your possessions when you leave this house, as I presume you will some day."

"Some day, Bernard."

There was a short silence, broken only by the sound of chewing.

"Gila monsters," mused Bernard, "have a bad reputation, but—"

"I've decided on a cat."

Maya cast a frightened glance at her husband. "Oh, Snooky, you *can't*."

"Why? What do you mean? Of course I can. I've always loved cats. You know that, Maya. I'm going to go out to the pound and get one tomorrow. I just thought I should warn you."

"Snooky, you don't understand. Bernard hates cats. You can't have a cat while you're staying here. How about a dog? Maybe Misty wouldn't be too jealous."

"I don't want a dog," Snooky said stubbornly. "I want a cat, and a cat I will get. Do you have a problem with that, Bernard?"

"No."

"Good. I mean, I wouldn't want to do anything that would upset you."

"It won't upset me."

"Good."

"I think you should get yourself a cat. It would suit you, Snooky. You're a cat kind of person."

"Thank you, Bernard."

"The only thing is, Snooky—"

"Yes?"

"Don't come back here with it."

Snooky looked hurt. "This is ridiculous. I mean, I've accepted that you can't stand people, but why cats? What have they ever done to you?"

"Nothing."

"So?"

Bernard did not reply. Maya said, "We'll talk about it later, okay, Snooks? Anyway, why do you have to have it right now? Why can't you get one when you leave?"

"I thought it would be nice to have one now. It's now that I need a little companionship, you know. Anyway, you love cats, Maya. Remember Snuffles?"

Maya's face melted. "Of course I remember Snuffles."

Snuffles had been her cat when she was little, a gray-and-white striped tiger cat with long fluffy hair that she had found wandering the streets near their home. Snuffles, under Maya's care, had been terribly spoiled and gotten unbelievably fat and lived to a dignified old age of eighteen. Even now the sight of a tiger-striped kitten could bring tears to Maya's eyes.

She cast an appraising look at her husband. "We'll talk about it later, all right, Snooky? Maybe Bernard will come around."

Bernard reached out a hand for the bread plate. "Clever of you to think of using Snuffles' memory," he remarked to Snooky.

"Thanks."

"You knew how she'd react, of course."

"Of course."

Bernard nodded thoughtfully and bit into a piece of bread. "Clever."

"I'm not saying yes," Maya said, bristling. "I just said we'd think about it."

"Thanks, Maya. One more thing. Is it okay if I invite Albert and Susan over for dinner sometime soon? I feel like I should do something for them, after Bella's death and all. You wouldn't mind, would you?"

Bernard's head snapped up. With a sound like a muffled roar, he shoved back his chair and left the room.

Maya watched him leave. "Snooky, honestly, your timing is terrible. First this crazy thing about the cat, and now inviting total strangers over to the house? Are you out of your mind?"

"I can't help it, My. I just like to push Bernard over the edge. It's so fascinating to see him react."

"You know he hates having people he doesn't know here."

"Maya, I have news for you. Bernard hates having people he *does* know here. Everybody except for you, as far as I can tell."

"But he doesn't even *know* the Whitakers."

"He met them at the funeral, didn't he? Maybe I should invite Aunt Etta too, he seemed to actually hit it off with her. What do you think?"

"I think," his sister said primly, "that you're just a hair's-breadth away from being packed up and evicted, Arthur Randolph."

Susan and Albert were standing in their mother's pink-and-gray bedroom, sorting through her possessions. They had put this task off for as long as possible, neither of them wanting to do it, but finally Susan came over and they spent the day putting clothes in Goodwill boxes and going through her correspondence. Albert, normally so good-tempered, was morose, and Susan, normally so energetic, looked tired and drained. They nearly had a shoving match over their mother's jewelry.

"You take it," Albert said, handing her the jewelry box. "It's yours, Susan."

"I don't want it. I said I don't *want* it, Albert."

"Well, I can't wear it. You take it."

"No. You keep it. Your wife can wear it someday."

"My wife?" Albert looked thoroughly startled. He shook his head, dropped his glasses, retrieved them from the

floor and polished them carefully on the doily which lay on his mother's dressing table. "Don't be silly. They're yours, Susie. I don't want to hear any more arguments."

"Oh, Albert." Susan opened the jewelry box and stared at the contents. The fiery stones glittered harshly, even in the subdued pink light of the bedroom. She lifted up the diamond-and-sapphire necklace that Bella had been wearing the night she died, and let it slip through her hand. She put the jewelry box down with a shudder.

"Horrible," she said. "Really horrible. Look, Albert, I'll take one or two little things, things I can wear, and I'll pick out some pieces for Aunt Etta. I know she's had her eye on one of Mother's bracelets for a while. I guess I could give this tiara to Dora, with her fixation on royalty, but it's really too valuable to give away. Maybe she could wear some of Mother's clothes instead. Is that too gruesome?"

She chose two necklaces and two bracelets, and they agreed to put the rest of the jewelry into a safe-deposit box. "I don't know why in the world Mother kept it around here anyway," Susan said. "Silly of her. Now, what else?"

Albert was gazing in mild despair at one of the closets. "How many clothes did she have, anyway? I don't remember her having so much."

"That's because you never notice clothes, Albert. Mother had a magnificent wardrobe."

"Do you want any of these?"

"Oh, yes, Albert. I'd love that sequined red silk evening gown. I can wear it to work at the *Ridgewood Star*. That should pop George's eyes right out of his head."

"Is that a no?"

"That's a no, Albert. I can't wear that stuff. Only Mother could pull it off."

Albert chewed thoughtfully on his lip. "How about Aunt Etta? Could she use any of this?"

"That just shows you how little you know about the important things in life, Albert. Etta wouldn't have a prayer of fitting into any of these clothes. She's too short and, well, fat."

"She's not fat. She's square. She's symmetrical: a perfect cube."

"All right, then, she's too short and cubical. I'll pack all these gowns up and give them away to some charity. There must be a charity for socialites who need evening gowns, don't you think? Is that finally it, then?"

"I think so. I'll have another look around." He left the room.

Susan was pulling dresses and skirts off their hangers and muttering furiously to herself when Albert returned, holding something long, black and furry in his arms. He held it out to her with distaste.

"Mother's mink coat. Disgusting thing. I hate these things. Do you know how many animals had to die to make this coat? Do you want it, Susie?"

"Not after that introduction." She went over and examined it. "It's still in perfect condition. I guess I'll just give it away with everything else. It's really a shame Aunt Etta can't wear this. Maybe I could have it altered to fit her. It could be a birthday present. Or even better, you know, I could give it to Mrs. MacGregor. I bet she'd *love* it, and she's just the right build: tall and thin, like Mother."

"Whatever you want, Susie."

Susan went back to the closet and ripped several gowns off their hangers. "Look at these clothes. What a waste," she said. "I could have bought ten outfits for the price she spent on one of these gowns. Twenty, maybe."

"Mother never counted the money she spent."

"Not on herself." Susan sounded bitter. She folded the clothes and stuffed them into an already overloaded box. "By the way, Albert, talking about birthday presents reminded me. We have to send out invitations to Aunt Etta's birthday party. You know she'd literally die of disappointment if we didn't do something for her eightieth. She's been talking about nothing else since last year."

"I know. I know. It's just such a *bad* time, Sue."

"Yes. Poor Aunt Etta. It couldn't have come at a worse time." She straightened up and put her hands on her hips. Her hair was escaping from the rubber band and curling madly around her face. She pushed it back with an impatient gesture. "Do you think Mrs. MacGregor would mind helping us out with the party? Would you mind asking her?"

"No, no, of course not. I'll ask her the next time she comes in."

"Good. Listen, Albert, I have to get home soon. Even Dora has a time limit with Harold. Last time she babysat, he tried to hit Pumpkin over the head with one of his toys."

"Which one?"

Susan regarded him with irritation. "What do you mean, which one? What difference does it make?"

"A lot of difference, Susie," he said vaguely. "If it was a pillow, for instance, that would be fine, but if it was a baseball bat, say, or that club he carries around sometimes—"

"Oh, Albert, you drive me crazy. Harold is a difficult child—I'm the first to admit that, aren't I?—but there's nothing really wrong with him. He's not a killer. Nobody in this family is a killer. *Nobody!*"

Albert stared at her, surprised by the vehemence in her tone. "Of course not, Susan. Don't be silly."

"*Nobody,*" she repeated to herself, and tore one of her mother's gowns angrily off its hanger.

The next day, Susan and Dora were sitting in Susan's tiny dining room after dinner. Susan was addressing the party invitations, and Dora was breastfeeding Pooh. Dora was gazing beatifically at some drawings that Harold had recently brought home and which Susan had taped up on the dining room wall. They showed a house, robin's-egg blue, and a buttercup yellow sun. There were trees around the house and a stick figure in a rust-colored outfit ("This is *you*, Mommy") in the yard.

"I don't think there's anything wrong with the boy at all," Dora said dreamily. Breastfeeding always made her feel warm and sleepy. "Look at those drawings. He's perfectly happy."

"He tried to kick a little girl in school today," said Susan, savagely addressing the envelopes.

"You wait and see. Harold is going to grow up into those fabulous looks of his. By the time he's a teenager he'll be an angel, a perfect angel."

"Dreamer," said Susan, and cocked her head toward her son's bedroom. "Did you hear anything? Is he asleep?"

"He's asleep. I went in there a while ago and he was out cold."

"Okay."

"You should have seen that handsome detective when I started feeding Pooh," Dora said. "He didn't know where to look. Men are so . . . so *priggish* about things like that."

"You love to make people uncomfortable that way, Dora. You know you do."

"It's true, Susie. I'm a devil, what can I say. The man thinks I'm an idiot, anyway. I talked to him about *Gilligan's Island* and he looked at me like I was scum."

"That's your act, Dora. Your stupid act. It doesn't mean anything."

"I guess not." Dora sighed and detached Pooh, who squalled briefly and then fell asleep, drooling. "I wish I could come to Aunt Etta's party, dear. I would give anything not to be going away that weekend."

"It's not going to be anything special. Just Albert and me and a few other people. We can't do anything big right now, not that Albert and I would have the faintest idea what we were doing if we tried to plan a big party. Where are you going away to?"

"Oh, we have to visit Phil's parents in Boston. You know how I feel about that. Phil's father always has a cold and he gives it to Pooh, and Phil's mother takes me aside and asks me if Phil's eating properly, he looks so thin and peaked. The last time I got so fed up I told her we were on a macrobiotic diet, just rice and seaweed and sometimes a little fish, and she believed me. She *believed* me, Susan."

"That's sad. You shouldn't tease her."

"And then she gives me her special recipe for pound cake. We've been to their house exactly twenty-four times in the six years that we've been married, and every single time she gives me her special recipe for pound cake. I wouldn't mind, but it isn't even a good recipe. Now Boston cream pie, *that* I could get excited about." She shifted the baby to her other arm. "So, when are you and George getting married?"

Susan made a face. "Please, Dora. Not for a while. Albert and I can't even plan a birthday party for Aunt Etta properly. How can we put together a wedding? George understands. He's not in any rush."

"What about Albert and that woman he's been seeing for a hundred years—Gretchen? What's going on with them?"

"I don't know. Albert never talks about her. I told him to keep some of Mother's jewels in case he ever got married, and he just looked at me like he didn't know who I was. It's a shame, because I like her. I think she'd be a good influence on him. By the way, Dora, you wouldn't have any use for a sequined red silk evening gown, would you? I have to get rid of all of Mother's clothes, and some of them are really stunning."

"Well, you know nobody loves dressing up more than I do, dear, but since Pooh here was born I'm lucky if I can stuff myself into a muumuu. Maybe in a year or two, if we decide not to have any more kids. Oh my God, what a thought. If I don't lose this weight before the next baby, they'll have to forklift me into the hospital."

"Well, maybe I'll hold onto some clothes for you. You're a little shorter than Mother, but you could have them altered. Unless you think it's too ghastly."

"Nothing's too ghastly that costs over two thousand dollars, dear. Which I presume this gown you're talking about did. Your mother always had great taste."

"I could give it to Gretchen, but it doesn't seem right somehow, not unless she and Albert make some definite plans."

"Oh, no, no, don't you *dare* give it to her, save it for me. In about five years, give or take a few, I'll have my figure back again, I promise. And all this talk of clothes reminds me. Did I tell you the latest about Princess Di? It seems she was out at this charity ball and . . ."

Susan listened patiently for a while. Finally she said, "Dora, dear, have I mentioned to you recently that I think this whole Princess Di thing is getting a little out of hand? I mean, in my opinion, it's not really *normal* anymore, if you don't mind my saying so?"

Dora airily waved a hand. "I know, Susie, I know. That's what Phil tells me too. But what *I* say is, why should I listen to somebody like Phil who lives and dies for *The Brady Bunch*? Anyhow, where was I? She was out at this fabulous all-star gala and . . ."

Mrs. MacGregor readily agreed to come in and "lend a hand," as she put it, for several days before the birthday party. She was, if the truth be known, genuinely fond of Aunt Etta. "I'd be glad to help," she told Albert. "Anything for you and Etta Pinsky."

"That's very kind of you, Mrs. MacGregor."

A little while later he came into the kitchen with the black coat bunched awkwardly in his arms. He held it out.

"Mother's mink coat," he said hesitantly, his face flushed. "Susan and I discussed it, and, well, she thought you might like it. If you don't mind. As kind of a thank-you for helping out. Susan thought—well, anyway . . . here it is." He thrust it toward her helplessly, reflecting how really *bad* he was at this kind of thing.

Mrs. MacGregor took the coat and held it reverently in her arms. Her old eyes filled with tears. Her wrinkled face seemed to pinch together and tremble.

"It's beautiful," she said, her voice shaking. "Beautiful. I never thought—I never thought that—" She wavered and threatened to break down completely. Albert wished fervently that he was dead. "Thank you," she managed at last. "It's lovely—just *lovely!*"

"You're very welcome," said Albert, and shambled hastily from the room.

That night Mrs. MacGregor went home to her little apartment on the edge of town with her heart full.

It was a bitterly cold day in late January, and she was wearing the mink coat. She got out of her car and, pulling it tightly around her, walked in a slow and stately fashion up her front walk.

She imagined the neighbors staring, peeking from behind their curtains and saying, "Look, there's Harriet MacGregor, with *the most fabulous black mink coat*—!"

She unlocked her door and went in. She walked over to her closet and began to take the coat off; then, hesitating, she pulled it back on. No need to take it off so soon, she thought. Not so soon. She could wear it a little while longer.

In fact, she wore it as she watched the evening news, then as she prepared her small dinner—just mashed potatoes and a little salad and a chicken leg, she never seemed to have much appetite anymore, even when she had cooked and cleaned for other people all day long. After dinner she made herself a nice cup of tea with milk and two lumps of sugar, and settled down in her favorite armchair to watch TV. She had taken off the coat while she ate dinner—she was afraid of spilling food on it—but now she pulled it across her knobby knees as a luxurious lap rug and stroked it happily as she watched a documentary about African wildlife.

She had always wanted to travel—although even when her husband Ian had been alive they had never had the money to go to Europe or Africa—and she watched eagerly as the camera panned across the African veldt. She lost herself in visions of giraffes moving majestically, their heads bobbing, across the plains. Elephant babies were so big, fancy that, she thought. So cute with their little trunks waving. A lion roared at the screen and she shook with a pleasurable twinge of fear. The lionesses hunted and the male of the species lay around all day stuffing himself on their spoils. She permitted herself a haughty sniff. Not unlike some human males she knew. Why, her friend Lottie had told her recently that old Mr. Thayer over on Cabbage Avenue had never worked *a day in his life* . . . !

It was somewhere between the new hospital show and the MacNeil/Lehrer report that her hand, gently stroking the dark mink fur, suddenly paused. Harriet MacGregor sat up straight in her chair, a bewildered look on her face.

"Well, now, that's odd. . . ." she said to herself. "Very odd . . . very odd indeed . . . I wonder why *that* would be—?"

The MacNeil/Lehrer NewsHour continued with a report about sperm whales, but Harriet MacGregor was no longer listening. She sat with her head cocked to one side, her mind slowly clicking over, a strange expression on her face.

Well, now, she thought. That really was *very* odd!

4

Mr. Whiskers looked proudly at his reflection in the mirror. His fur was white and soft, his feet were pink and sturdy, and his whiskers— his pride and joy—were long, white and curled in a devil-may-care manner at the ends. "Hurrah!" he cried. "I am the handsomest rat in Ratdom!"

Bernard stopped typing and put his head down on his desk. He felt himself to be dangerously close to tears. For crying out loud, the handsomest rat in Ratdom! He lay there for a while, his head cradled in his arms, thinking long weary thoughts.

It was pitch dark in the study where he sat. He worked best in the dark. Many of his finest works, including his most popular book of all, *Mrs. Woolly and the Bengal Tiger*, had been conceived and executed in the dark. He was an expert in touch-typing and could keep up to one and a half pages at a time in his head. He found, more and

more, that it interfered with his creative work if he could actually see what he was doing. When the sunlight filtered through the closed blinds, filling the room with a pale diffuse light, he would often type with his eyes closed.

Now he felt close to despair. He could not concentrate on his work at all. Visions of talking rodents and intelligent sheep danced the tarantella in his head. He lay there, his eyes closed, his brain weary and confused.

Suddenly the lights were switched on, and a voice said, "Ah, Bernard. Work going well?"

Bernard sat up. "Just fine."

"Taking a little break?"

"I was just thinking over a few small details," Bernard said coldly.

Snooky sat down and smiled at him over the clutter.

Bernard's desk was a massive cherrywood antique that Maya had found in a dusty little store in Vermont. It was covered with books, papers, quick sketches of rats and sheep, erasers, pencils, pens, giant paper clips which Bernard had once (in a moment of idleness) linked together into a fifteen-foot chain, one of Misty's old flea collars, and a small silver-framed photo of Maya.

"How's it going, Bernard?"

"Fine, thank you."

"I am here to tell you something which will fill your heart with joy. I have just received an invitation to Aunt Etta's eightieth birthday party, and guess what?"

Bernard did not show any inclination to guess.

"You're invited, too. You must have made quite an impression on her at that reception, eh, Bernard? Well, what do you say? Will you go?"

Bernard regarded him thoughtfully. "Ordinarily I wouldn't go. You know that."

"But you'll go this time?"

"No. Of course not. But I want you to go. And keep your eyes open, Snooky. You know as well as I do that one of the people at that party probably murdered your friend."

"Don't worry about me, Bernard. I'm like a cat."

Bernard flinched at the mention of the hated word. "What do you mean?"

"I always land on my feet."

"Cats don't always land on their feet. It's a myth."

"No, really? Is that true?"

"Yes."

"How would you know that, Bernard?"

"There are a lot of myths about cats. That they make good pets, for instance. The only good pets are dogs."

"I don't agree."

"I don't have time to argue with you about it, Snooky.

Just take my word for it. And if you're going to go to this party, try to be careful. Your sister is worried enough about you as it is."

Snooky smiled cheerfully. "Oh, I'll be careful. I'm always careful. And I'll keep my eyes open, like you said. Who knows, maybe I'll see something important."

"Somehow I doubt that very much," said Bernard sourly.

Snooky wandered into the next room. This was Maya's study. Like Bernard's, it looked out over the back lawn through tall, narrow windows, but there the resemblance ended. Whereas Bernard's study was small, dominated by the big old desk and cluttered with books, papers and oddments, Maya's study was clean, light and airy. She worked at an antique pine table covered with dark knobbly whorls. The room itself was big and square, the wallpaper was sprigged in blue and violet flowers, and a glowing Turkish rug lay on the hardwood floor. Snooky sank with a sigh of relief into the overstuffed armchair.

Maya looked up from her word processor. "What is it, Snooks? Be brief. I have an article due tomorrow."

"What's it on?"

"Quetzals."

"What's that?"

"*Pharomachrus mocino*, you dumbhead. A Central American bird. I have to write three thousand words on its feeding habits by tomorrow morning. Kindly state your purpose, then get out."

Snooky explained about the party and Bernard's refusal. "But you're welcome to come if you want, Maya."

"Thank you, but no. And I wish you'd forget it too, Snooks. I think it's dangerous to get too friendly with those people."

"It is not. Don't be ridiculous."

"I'm not being ridiculous. I'm being practical, a virtue I have in common with William, one which you apparently never inherited. Listen to me, Snooky. You're an adult now and I can't tell you what to do, but I wish you wouldn't go. You know it's not safe."

"Please, Maya. Don't do this. Nobody is out to get me, after all."

"They might be if they thought you saw something," she said shrewdly. "And the longer you hang around with them, the more likely it is that you *will* see something."

Snooky looked away. "Bella was my friend."

She looked at him. Snooky's face was set in the stubborn expression she remembered so well from his childhood— the expression she referred to as his you're-not-the-boss-of-*me* face. She sighed. It was true, she was not the boss of him. She wondered briefly whether she ever had been. Out loud she said:

"Yes. I do understand, Snookers. You go to that party and have yourself a good time."

Mrs. MacGregor was cackling merrily to herself as she got the broom out of the closet. Aunt Etta said sharply,

"What is it, woman? What's so funny?"

Mrs. MacGregor cast a sly eye at her. "Nothing."

"Then why all the giggling?"

MacGregor shook her head mutely and set to work with unaccustomed vigor. Aunt Etta watched critically.

"You've missed that spot over there," she said at last, in triumph. "And over there. Honestly, sometimes I wonder why I hire you, MacGregor. You do a lousy job."

Ordinarily MacGregor would have bristled at this, and demanded a full apology and a rest break before she went on. Etta waited in anticipation. Instead, MacGregor simply smiled, shook her head and laughed. Etta felt vaguely annoyed. She drummed her fingers on the sink and said gruffly, "Cup of tea?"

Yes, thank you, said Mrs. MacGregor. A cup of tea would be very nice.

The two old women were sitting around the table gossiping, as usual, when Aunt Etta said, "I heard from Susan that she gave you Bella's mink coat. Is that right?"

Oh, yes, said Mrs. MacGregor. And a lovely coat it was, too.

"Beautiful," said Aunt Etta. "I remember her wearing it. I'm glad you took it, MacGregor; it wouldn't fit me, I'm too short. So you like it, do you?"

MacGregor looked vastly pleased. Oh, yes, she said. It was so beautiful, that coat. And there was something else . . . something else it had brought to mind that perhaps she ought to mention. . . .

"What?"

MacGregor opened her mouth, then closed it abruptly and sat looking at Aunt Etta with a very strange expression on her face. She shook her head slowly from side to side.

Nothing, she replied. Nothing. Except that that detective who was all puffed up with himself the other day wasn't as smart as he made himself out to be.

"What are you gibbering about, MacGregor?"

MacGregor gave a haughty sniff. The way he asked her whether she had left by the front door or not! Goodness! Why, if he knew what *she* knew . . .

"What is it, MacGregor? What do you know?"

MacGregor looked at her craftily. Nothing, she said. She didn't know anything. Or rather, she knew something, but it didn't make any sense.

Aunt Etta knew that MacGregor was deliberately withholding some piece of delicious gossip. It put her in a snappish mood.

"That doesn't surprise me, MacGregor. Half the things you talk about never do make any sense. I told you to stop pretending you knew something about my niece's death, now didn't I? You'll do anything for a little attention. Now, what do you think Susan gave *me* from Bella's estate, eh?"

Mrs. MacGregor leaned forward eagerly and said that she couldn't imagine. The talk turned to a lively discussion of the ruby-and-silver bracelet that Susan had picked out for Aunt Etta. . . .

A few days later, Jessie Lowell was sitting on her living room floor, surrounded by boxes, wrapping paper, ribbon, and tape. She was holding a flat rectangular box, folding the wrapping paper this way and that, and murmuring,

"Oh, *dear* . . . oh, dear, I *knew* I should have asked Gretch to . . . oh, my, now how does that go? Let's see, a little bit of Scotch tape here, just to hold it while I fold this over . . . oh! Oh, *damn*!" The paper had torn. "Oh, dear, I'll just have to start all over again . . . what a *mess* . . . !"

In the kitchen, Gretchen was delivering a strict lecture to Mrs. MacGregor. "Now, Mrs. MacGregor," she was saying, not unkindly, "I know I asked you to make chicken parmesan, not eggplant parmesan, for dinner tonight. Isn't that so? And now here you've made the eggplant. It's not that it matters, it's just that your mind doesn't seem to be on your cooking today."

Mrs. MacGregor was looking disgruntled. "I'm sure I don't know what you mean. I heard you say eggplant parmesan as plain as plain can be. If you don't want it, I'll whip up some chicken for you and Miss Lowell—"

"No, no, don't be silly. I just wondered—is something wrong?" She looked at the old woman anxiously. Help was so hard to get, and Mrs. MacGregor was usually so reliable. . . .

Mrs. MacGregor simpered at her in a singularly unbecoming manner. "Nothing's wrong. Nothing at all. On the contrary. There's just a few things I've been thinking over in my mind. Just a few things having to do with poor Mrs. Whitaker and the way she went. . . ."

"Mrs. Whitaker?"

Yes, said Mrs. MacGregor. It was sad to die that young, wasn't it? Mrs. Whitaker was only sixty-eight, while she, Mrs. MacGregor, was a good seven years older.

Gretchen felt a wrenching pang of guilt. So Mrs. MacGregor was seventy-five, and here she was cooking and cleaning for two women in the prime of their lives? She looked at the older woman doubtfully. Perhaps she ought to suggest retirement—something in the nature of a pension fund . . . she wasn't very good at business, but perhaps . . .

"Have you ever thought about retirement?"

Mrs. MacGregor looked insulted. Retirement! No, indeed! She wouldn't know what to do with herself if she wasn't working. She hoped Dr. Schneider didn't think she was hinting anything, with all this talk about her age. That wasn't what she had meant.

Gretchen said hastily, oh, no, of course not . . .

"Did you know that Dr. Whitaker gave me a coat?" Mrs. MacGregor asked. "A beautiful black mink that his mother used to wear?"

"No," Gretchen said absently. "A mink coat? Isn't that nice. Actually, yes, I think Albert said something about it."

"Yes," said Mrs. MacGregor. She looked at Gretchen and lowered her voice in a stealthy way. "I was *there*, you know—actually *in the house*—the evening that It happened. . . ."

"Terrible for you," Gretchen said even more abstractedly, as Jessie bustled into the kitchen. She was carrying the flat box in her arms.

"Look, Gretch, I mean, it's hopeless," she said. "I can't get it right. It's not any good, is it?"

Gretchen and Mrs. MacGregor looked at the present. The wrapping paper, a lively design of hearts engraved with *Happy Birthday* and little cakes with candles, was coiled round and round the package as if around an Egyptian mummy. Blue and red ribbons hung limply from the center, stuck on with a gluey mountain of Scotch tape.

"The wrapping paper you chose is beautiful," Gretchen said kindly. "But no, it doesn't seem quite right the way it is. Perhaps we should try it again, Jess, the two of us."

"I'm just no good at this kind of thing," Jessie said in despair as they left the kitchen. Behind them, Mrs. MacGregor cackled meanly to herself, then turned back to the much-debated eggplant parmesan.

It was the day before the birthday party, and Susan was in a frenzy. She ran to and fro between the kitchen of the Whitaker mansion—where the cake was being delivered, the champagne unloaded, and the punch stirred together—and the living room, which was festooned with garlands of flowers, crepe paper and a large sign that said in gold letters, HAPPY 80TH BIRTHDAY, AUNT ETTA. George, standing outside the kitchen door, was shouting at the men who had brought the champagne.

"No, no, no, don't put it there, put it over *there*—we can't leave it outdoors, it'll freeze—" He shook his head and dug his hands into the pockets of his coat. It was three degrees below zero. The delivery men wore light blue jackets and seemed perfectly comfortable. "Over there," George said, raising his voice. "Leave the champagne in here, in the corner of the kitchen—watch out, Mrs. MacGregor—"

Mrs. MacGregor uttered a startled yelp as three delivery men landed a crate near her left foot. She said a few earnest, heartfelt words to them and the men, sensing *real* authority, backed away.

Susan came into the kitchen and examined the cake box critically. "Do you think it's big enough? It's double chocolate. You know how Aunt Etta loves chocolate, George.

I got it from Betsey's Bakery, they're the best in town. Should I take a peek? Oh, God, it looks fabulous. Good. That's a load off my mind. What else do we have to do?"

"I wanted to talk to you about the music," said George. "The music is all-important at an event like this. Trust me. It makes all the difference. I thought I'd start with a little piece by Bach, transposed for viola, and then maybe a little gem by Schubert I think your aunt will like—"

"Just as long as you play 'Happy Birthday,' Georgie, when Etta comes into the room. Please, Georgie, *please* try to remember that this is a birthday party, not a performance. Play 'Happy Birthday' so we can all sing along, okay? Then something catchy, like maybe a show tune or something. Do you know any jazz?"

"Jazz?"

"Aunt Etta loves jazz. You wouldn't think it to look at her, but she does. Isn't that true, Mrs. MacGregor?"

From her position, ramrod-straight, at the stove, Mrs. MacGregor remarked sourly that Etta Pinsky loved jazz.

"You see, George. So there. All right, what else is there to do? Why don't we go into the living room and you can play 'Happy Birthday' for me?"

"I know how to play 'Happy Birthday,' " George said, offended. He picked up one of the little pink frosted cakes Mrs. MacGregor was baking for the next day, and shoved it into his mouth. "Mmmmmm, *delicious*. You know, I have a recipe for *spanakopita* that you could die for, Susan. No party should be without *spanakopita*. I could whip up a few pans of it for tomorrow—"

"No, George." Susan took his arm and guided him out of the room. "You're not here to cook. You have enough on your mind with the music. I want you to be able to enjoy this party, too. Do you think it's macabre to have it here, where the funeral reception was? Is it unlucky? Is it tempting fate?"

George looked at her with affection. Susan's hair was, as usual, escaping from its clip and frizzing around her head in a red-gold halo. There were blue shadows under her eyes that he had not noticed before, but otherwise her face looked as always: round and cheerful and glowing with energy.

"No, no, it's not tempting fate." He put his arms around her. "And I'd play 'Happy Birthday' a hundred times for Aunt Etta if you wanted me to, Susie."

"All right, George. Just no *spanakopita*, okay? Mrs. MacGregor would never forgive me for letting somebody else cook. She's already upset over the birthday cake." She put her arms around his neck and kissed him warmly.

Albert came around the corner and started nervously at seeing them together. He beat a hasty retreat toward the kitchen, where Mrs. MacGregor simpered at him and offered him a plate of frosted cakes. Albert looked around doubtfully at the party preparations.

"It doesn't seem right, does it, Mrs. MacGregor? So soon after . . . well, you know."

Mrs. MacGregor was, surprisingly, not sympathetic. She clucked her tongue and said that she didn't know whether it was or not. It was more important to celebrate than to grieve, she added, rather poetically.

"Speaking of that night, though," she said, "the night It happened . . . you know, there's something I just realized . . . something that I saw, or rather, *didn't* see, if you take my meaning—"

"No, I don't, Mrs. MacGregor. What do you mean?"

Mrs. MacGregor sidled closer to him and said that it was just something she should have seen that she didn't . . . something that should have been there, but wasn't. . . .

Albert said sharply, "What are you talking about, Mrs. MacGregor?"

There was laughter from the hallway and Susan and George came into the room together. Mrs. MacGregor was covered with confusion. Blushing, she retired to the counter near the oven and busied herself with the cakes.

"No, Georgie, I don't think it's appropriate for you to play that three-hour piece you wrote for solo viola," Susan was saying. "And I *do* think we need to move some of the chairs closer together in the living room. We'll put Etta in the middle. Hello, Albert, when did you get home?"

Mrs. MacGregor mumbled an excuse and left the room. "Just a few minutes ago," Albert said, gazing worriedly after her.

"What is it?"

"I don't know, Susie. Something Mrs. MacGregor saw . . . or didn't see. . . . I don't know. You know how she loves to hint about things."

"The woman lives for gossip," Susan said acidly. She bent to examine the champagne. "Oh, yes, this will be terrific."

Albert was still looking pensively out the kitchen door. "You know, I wonder if she really does know something. Maybe I should call the police and let them talk to her. What do you think, Susie?"

"Oh, it's nothing, Albert. It's nothing at all. You know how she is."

"Yes," said Albert slowly. "Yes, I'm sure you're right."

"So you're off to your little party?" Maya said as Snooky came downstairs. He was wearing a dark jacket and a pearl gray tie which belonged to Bernard.

"I'm off."

"Isn't that jacket a little too big for you?"

"I think it looks stylish, My." Snooky paused in front of the hallway mirror and adjusted his tie.

"Don't you ever get tired of borrowing Bernard's clothes? They don't really fit you, you know."

"No, Maya. I love Bernard's wardrobe. He has two identical ties and two identical jackets. I've never seen anything like it. Doesn't he ever go out?"

"You know he doesn't, Snooky."

"Well, at least his clothes should. And it allows me to travel light when I'm coming here."

Bernard came into the hallway and glanced at his brother-in-law. "Nice jacket," he said sadly.

"Thank you, Bernard."

"That tie also looks familiar."

"That's not surprising. You have two of them."

"Please have them home by midnight."

"I'll do my best. Well, so long. Don't wait up for me. You know these eightieth birthday parties can get pretty wild."

"So long, Snooks." Maya opened the door for him. "Have a good time. And Snooky—"

"Yes?"

"Try not to get murdered."

Aunt Etta sat proudly, her legs dangling, in a big armchair in the middle of the living room. All around her people were talking, laughing, and drinking punch or champagne. George, in the corner, was playing an impromptu variation and fugue on the theme from 'Happy Birthday.'

Susan said, "Here you are, Aunt Etta. This is from Harold and me."

Etta eagerly ripped open the small package. Inside was a gold necklace with a tiny gold heart pendant. Susan helped her put it on.

"It's very nice, Susie, thank you. Haul your son over here and I'll give him a kiss."

Susan looked around, but Harold was busy elsewhere. He and Snooky were having a face-off in the corner.

"I don't like you," Harold said loudly.

"Well, I don't like you, either."

"I think I'll bite your leg."

"You do that and you're going to have some severe problems."

"I think I'll bite your arm."

"You sound hungry. How about one of these little cakes instead?"

Susan came up and put her arm around Harold. "Is he being good?" she asked Snooky.

"Just as good as he can be."

Susan departed, satisfied. Snooky said, "You know, my brother-in-law writes books for cute little tykes like you. Have you read any of his Mrs. Woolly books?"

"No."

"How about Mr. Whiskers?"

"No."

"Do you read? I mean, anything besides *Modern Mercenary?*"

"No."

"That's nice," said Snooky. "Excuse me, there are some people over there I have to talk to now."

Etta was opening the present that Gretchen and Jessie had brought. Jessie hovered nearby, saying anxiously, "I hope you like it . . . we thought about it for a long time and . . . oh, let me help you with the Scotch tape. . . . I knew we put on too much—there! Do you like it?"

Aunt Etta lifted it from the box. It was a spring dress in a pale rose color. It had lace at the neck, and swirled out from the waist in soft gathers.

Aunt Etta nodded approvingly. "It's beautiful."

"Do you really think so?" gushed Jessie.

"Yes, yes, yes. Now, what's next?"

Snooky handed her a small box. "It's from all three of us. Bernard, Maya, and me. It's a little sentimental, but I think you'll like it."

Aunt Etta pinched his cheek, then opened the box. Inside was a charm bracelet with one single charm hanging from it. Aunt Etta held it up close to her eye. The charm was a tiny golden replica of a tractor.

Aunt Etta let out a shriek and began to shake with silent, delighted laughter.

In the kitchen, Mrs. MacGregor was humming quietly to herself. The party was a great success. Nearly all the champagne was gone, and the cake had been finished to the last crumb. So had her little pink cakes. She permitted herself a smug smile. Betsey's Bakery, indeed! Susan should have asked *her* to make the birthday cake. She had a recipe for a double chocolate fudge cake that would have put Betsey's to shame. . . .

There was a sound behind her and she turned, startled. Then she smiled a pleased welcome. "Oh, hello. How are you?"

"Just fine, thanks."

"How is the party going?"

"Oh, fine, fine. They're calling for you in there, Mrs. MacGregor. Aunt Etta wants to see you."

"Really?" MacGregor wiped her hands on her apron,

then took it off and hung it neatly on its hook. She felt a surge of pleased excitement. "Was it my cakes?"

"Oh, yes. The cakes were wonderful. Everybody says so."

"My secret recipe," MacGregor said smugly. "Wait a minute. I really should put these dishes away before I go—"

She bent over the dish rack where the newly washed dishes were propped together. Behind her there was a sudden movement. Mercifully, she never knew anything. She felt a sudden pain and then pitched forward into blackness. . . .

5

Detective Janovy looked at Susan's tightly drawn face and said, "Go on, Miss Whitaker."

"There's nothing more to tell." She glared at him, almost defiantly. She was sitting curled up in one of the big chairs in the Whitaker living room. George sat next to her, on the sofa. Wrapping paper and bright ribbons and presents were scattered all over the floor. The golden sign HAPPY 80TH BIRTHDAY, AUNT ETTA still hung from the ceiling. The setting was as inappropriate for a murder investigation, Janovy felt, as it could possibly be.

Mrs. MacGregor's body had been discovered by Albert at nine o'clock, as the party was starting to wind down. He had gone into the kitchen to get more champagne, and had found Mrs. MacGregor face down on the floor in a pool of her own blood. A ten-inch kitchen knife, snatched from the rack of knives over the counter, was buried squarely in the middle of her back. Albert had reacted as if this sort of thing happened to him all the time, which in fact it was beginning to. He had gone straight to the phone and called the police. Then he had gone back into the living room and said, "I'm afraid something terrible has happened."

The police had arrived fifteen minutes later. Janovy had spoken to everyone except Susan, who had taken her son to Dora's house and then come back ("I can't have Harold here," she had said in her practical way, before bundling him into the car), and Albert himself.

Now he was trying to interview Susan, but it wasn't easy.

"Mrs. MacGregor was talking to your brother when you came into the kitchen yesterday?"

"That's right. I've already told you so."

"And she was saying—?"

Susan made an impatient gesture. "I don't remember exactly what it was. Do you, George?"

George sat clutching his viola and bow. His face had the same anxious, unhappy expression as Susan's. "I don't know. Susie and I had just come in. She was saying something to Albert, but she stopped when she saw us."

Susan said impatiently, "Mrs. MacGregor was always going on about something—oh, I know it's terrible to say, but it's true. She loved to gossip, to blow things out of proportion. I've learned not to pay any attention."

But this time, thought Janovy, you were wrong, weren't you? As if she knew what he was thinking, she stared at him defiantly and said,

"This time I should have listened. But how was I to *know*?"

Albert said calmly, "What next, Detective? What next?"

He was sitting in the dining room at the great mahogany table. The room was ornate, with oil paintings on the walls, a Calder mobile hanging from the vaulted ceiling, and heavy blue silk curtains. Gretchen sat next to him, his hand in hers. Jessie had had a fit when the body was discovered, and after hysterically claiming total ignorance of anything having to do with murder in general and this murder in particular, she had been allowed by the police to go home.

Janovy looked at Albert sharply. He seemed calm and composed; too composed, thought Janovy. It wasn't natural.

"Please, Dr. Whitaker, just tell me what Mrs. MacGregor was saying to you yesterday."

Albert said vaguely, "It was something to do with something she saw the night my mother was killed . . . I'm not quite sure . . . she could have meant anything, really. She said there was something she just realized— something she should have seen but didn't, or might have seen but couldn't, or would have seen but hadn't. . . . Is that helpful, Detective?"

Janovy, remembering Palomino Grove and mushrooms, rose to his feet.

"Do you have anything to add, Dr. Schneider?"

Gretchen jumped a bit. "Oh, no, no, of course not. I wasn't here yesterday. I told you already that Mrs. MacGregor had been hinting around to all of us. You know, Detective, we want to be helpful, but Albert's had an awful shock, and I think he should go lie down for a while. I mean, all this happening right after his mother's death—you understand how we feel—"

"Yes. Just one more thing, Dr. Whitaker. Was there anything else unusual about Mrs. MacGregor's behavior in the past few days?"

Albert took his glasses off and polished them assiduously on the table linen. With the glasses off, his face looked less moon-eyed and more sensitive than ever. Janovy could see that it was marked with deep lines which seemed to have come all at once, recently. Albert said thoughtfully, "There's the coat, of course."

"The coat?"

Albert explained. "She was the right height for it, you see . . . at least, that's what Susan said—you know," he said abruptly, "it's not Susan's fault that I didn't call the police yesterday. I hope she didn't make it out that it was."

"What do you mean?"

"Oh . . . well . . ." He explained that he had wanted to go to the police, but his sister had stopped him. "But it's not her fault. I should have called anyway. After all, Mrs. MacGregor was talking to *me*."

Janovy cast a look over his shoulder at Fish, who was sitting nearby taking notes. So Susan had stopped her brother from calling the police, had she? Fish's face showed no emotion at all. His eyes were bulging, but then Fish's eyes always bulged. Janovy said, "I see. Yes. Where is the coat now?"

"It's here, in the front closet. She—Mrs. MacGregor wore it here today. She was very proud of it, I think."

Janovy thought this over. Perhaps it was something about the coat . . . or something *missing* from the coat. . . .

"Thank you, Dr. Whitaker. If you don't mind, we'll take the coat with us when we leave. Thank you for your cooperation."

"You're welcome."

On the way out, Janovy stopped at the front closet and opened it. There, hanging in the center, was the mink coat. Janovy took it out and looked it over carefully. Nothing out of the ordinary. Nice quality, he thought. Nothing obviously missing.

He felt in the pockets. Nothing there. He draped it over one arm and said, "Come along, Fish."

". . . so the poor old woman was stabbed to death in the kitchen while the rest of us were out partying and giving birthday presents," said Snooky.

"Not all of you," said Bernard.

"What?"

"Not all of you were out partying when Mrs. MacGregor was killed."

"No." Snooky moved restlessly in his chair. He looked pale and drained; he had lost weight recently and his cheekbones stood out sharply on his face. "No, I guess not."

Bernard had ushered his brother-in-law into his study and for the past hour had been grilling him relentlessly about the birthday party. Who was where, who talked to whom, and most importantly, who left the room and when. . . .

Snooky, as it turned out, had an excellent memory for these kinds of things. His account was detailed and lucid, but not, in the end, particularly helpful. People had been coming and going all evening, and it was impossible to pin down exactly when Mrs. MacGregor had been killed. She had been found at nine o'clock, the police were there by nine-fifteen, and Snooky had heard them say the death could have occurred anytime between seven-thirty and eight-thirty.

"Who left the room then?"

Snooky lifted an eyebrow. "Contrary to your expectations, Bernard, I wasn't sitting with my eyes glued to my watch the entire time. I don't know. Let's see . . . Albert went out at one point to get more punch . . . Gretchen

was going back and forth to the kitchen, helping out . . .
Susan was running herself ragged. . . . Well, I really don't
know."

Bernard looked at him coldly. "So much for keeping
your eyes open, eh?"

"I'm sorry. What can I say? If you want my personal
opinion, I think that kid Harold did it. There's something
actively evil about him. Have you noticed this?"

Bernard was not interested. He was gazing out of the
window into darkness.

Snooky sat with his forehead wrinkled. "As far as I can
tell, the only person who never left the room, even once,
was Aunt Etta. She came in at five o'clock, sat down in a
chair in the middle of the room and never budged. And
Susan's friend George was in the room most of the time,
too. I remember because he was playing some incredibly
long piece he wrote himself, and Susan kept asking him to
stop."

"So Mrs. MacGregor had been hinting about something—
something she saw or didn't see?"

"Yes. To nearly everybody, it turns out. Aunt Etta told
me that Mrs. MacGregor was never happier than when
she had a secret like that. She could spin it out for days.
Of course, in this case she didn't get much of a chance."
Despite his flippant tone, Snooky looked depressed. He
slouched in his chair, fiddling idly with a rubber band he
had unearthed from the clutter on top of Bernard's desk.

"Could anyone else have gotten into the house—maybe
through the back door, into the kitchen?"

"That's the first thing the police checked for. All the
doors and windows were locked on the inside. It's got to
be someone who was at that party, Bernard."

"Looks like it. Five people, then, assuming you're
right about Aunt Etta never leaving the room."

"Yes."

"Six people, counting you."

A wan smile broke over Snooky's face. "Thank you. Thank you so much, Bernard. Your trust is a rare and beautiful thing."

"Stop twanging that rubber band," said Bernard. "Go lie down. You look awful. And Snooky—"

"Yes?"

"Turn off the lights when you leave."

After Snooky had departed, Bernard sat quietly in the darkness for a while. Then he switched on his desk lamp, took out a small notebook and fished around in the top drawer for a large green Magic Marker. He opened the notebook and wrote in his neat, cramped hand,

SMTHNG SH DDNT C?

"Something she didn't see?" he said out loud, and grunted to himself. Bernard had developed his own private shorthand for taking notes. It was his firm belief that vowels were not required for reading comprehension. The fact that he had often been proved tragically wrong, as when he was unable to decipher his own notes later, had never dampened his enthusiasm.

Underneath he wrote:

CT?

This looked very much like the abbreviation for Connecticut, but in fact stood for *coat*. He stared at that for a while.

Under that he wrote:

$$

and underlined it heavily.
     Then:

GRD

and

MRRG

     "Greed," he said out loud, and grunted cheerfully.
"Marriage."
     Bernard had always made a curious grunting sound
when his work was going well. Now the only sound in his
study was the dog's snoring and his happy porcine grunts
as his hand traveled down the page, noting points and
questions for future investigation. . . .

     Maya came into Snooky's bedroom and sat down on
the edge of the bed. Outdoors, it was five degrees Fahren-
heit; in the third-floor guest bedroom, it felt like it was ten
below. She said, "Good Lord, Snooky, how does it get so
cold in here?"
     "I don't know, My." He was sitting up, wrapped in a
thick cocoon of blankets, leaning against a pile of pillows.
"I don't understand it myself. Ask Bernard."
     She regarded him quietly. He held a rubber band
between his fingers and was plucking at it listlessly.
     "Snooky."
     "Yes?"
     "I won't say I told you so."
     "Thank you, Maya. Thank you more than I can ever say."

"Can I get you anything?"

"No. No. I'll just sit here and freeze to death. Please tell Bernard he can go out and dance on my grave."

"Something hot, maybe?"

"Well . . . a cup of tea would be nice."

A few minutes later she returned with a steaming cup of tea. "With milk and honey. Just the way you like it."

"Thanks, My. You're too good to me."

"I turned up the heat."

"What?"

"I turned up the heat."

"Oh, don't do that, Maya. You'll take away Bernard's only joy in life. You know he loves to watch me suffer."

"I think you're going through enough without having to freeze," Maya said mildly. "Want to talk about it?"

"No. No, I don't. Thank you."

"Sure?"

"Yes. It's just . . . Maya?"

"Still here, Snooky."

"I want to get whoever's behind this. I want to find out who it is, and then I want to bring him in. It's not right, Maya. I'm telling you, it's not right."

She regarded him with concern. His face was set in that stubborn attitude she knew so well. "Snooky—"

"Yes?"

He had lost so much weight recently, she thought. As unreliable as he generally was, one thing you had to say about him was that he was a loyal friend. She knew he had not been sleeping well. Sometimes in the middle of the night she would wake up and hear the television on downstairs. Whenever he was depressed, he would watch TV. "TV is my friend," he would say, flicking the dial.

"I don't think there's anything I can say."

"I guess not."

"Just watch out for yourself."

"Don't worry about me, Maya. I'm like a cat."

"Oh, *please*."

"Anyway, you should worry about Bernard instead. He's been thinking about this thing, too."

"I don't have to worry about Bernard," Maya said tartly. "He'll never get killed."

"How do you know?"

"Because he never leaves the house, Snooky. Now, can I make you something nice and hot to eat?"

"No fingerprints on the knife?" Janovy asked.

Fish shook his head. "No, sir. None besides Mrs. MacGregor's anyway. Hers were there, faintly blurred. We found this—" he produced a red-and-blue checked kitchen towel—"on the counter nearby. The killer must have wrapped it around his hand before picking up the knife."

"*His* hand, Fish?"

"Or hers, of course."

"Would this have taken a great deal of strength?"

"No. The knife was sharp. A woman could easily have done it."

Janovy nodded. "How about the coat? Has it been examined?"

"Yes, sir. Nothing out of the ordinary, as far as we could see. The pockets were empty; nothing was missing from the coat itself. So what she said about not seeing something—"

"Doesn't apply to something on the coat. All right, Fish. Thank you."

Philip West said dryly, "Two murders and no clues?"

"That's right, sir. Or next to no clues."

"Any particular suspicions?"

"No, sir."

Philip West regarded Detective Janovy with an appraising look. "Tell me about it."

Philip West was the head of the Detective Bureau in the Ridgewood Police Department. He was a big barrel-chested man with a rumbling laugh. He was not laughing now. He listened thoughtfully as Janovy went over the case. When Janovy was finished, Philip West said,

"Look, Paul. You're at a dead end right now. That doesn't mean anything. You keep digging, and something will turn up. It always does. You've got a small group of people there, and remember, there are no murders without clues. No one is *that* clever."

Janovy nodded, but inside he wondered to himself. Was that invariably true? He had a feeling he was dealing with someone who was cleverer than most. . . .

Harold was jumping rope on the back porch. "One hunnerd one," he said in triumph. "One hunnerd two, one hunnerd three—"

Susan came to the back door and said, "That's enough, Harold. It's time for lunch."

"One hunnerd six, one hunnerd seven—"

"Harold!"

"One hunnerd nine, one hunnerd ten . . ."

Susan held the door open and Harold skipped in, his cheeks flaming red from the cold and the exercise. "One hunnerd *twelve*," he crowed, and put the rope away. "One hunnerd twelve, Mommy!"

"That's wonderful, dear."

Over lunch, which consisted of a peanut butter and banana sandwich with a big glass of grape juice, Harold stopped his loud chewing and said, "Mommy?"

"Yes, dear?"

"You know the night that Granny was killed?"

Susan leaned forward and touched his arm gently. It was the first time he had spoken of it. "Yes, dear?"

"I was listening at the door when you were talking to that detective about it," he said frankly.

"Oh, *Harold*!"

"And I don't remember Aunt Dora coming over that night."

"The night Granny died?"

He nodded solemnly.

Susan stared at him, puzzled. "Oh, don't be silly, Harold. Of course she did. It was a few weeks ago, anyway. Why should you remember?"

"Well, I don't remember it."

"Your Aunt Dora visits us all the time, darling. How could you remember whether or not she was here that particular night?"

"Well . . . I guess not."

Susan poured him more fruit juice, but he pushed the glass away. "Can I jump rope some more?"

"All right. Whatever you want."

Harold ran to the corner for the rope, then skipped off madly down the hall, chanting (with a shocking lack of veracity that would have disqualified him from any official jump rope competition), "One hunnerd *thirteen*, one hunnerd *fourteen* . . ."

Susan remained at the kitchen counter, her forehead furrowed.

*   *   *

"Jessie, we have to put our thinking caps on."

"What do you mean, Gretch?"

"I mean, we have to put our heads together and think everything over very carefully. We were *there* the other day, weren't we? There must have been something—some clue or another that one of us saw—"

"Like what?"

"It could be something very minor," Gretchen said. "Like somebody left the room for a minute and came back with their face all flushed, or acted a little oddly—"

"I don't think anybody would do that," Jessie said unexpectedly. "If you committed a murder, wouldn't you try to act just as normal as possible afterwards? *I* certainly would."

"Yes—I see what you mean. Well, that's no help then."

"Unless we can think of somebody who was acting *more* normal than usual."

"Oh, don't be silly, Jessie. That doesn't mean anything. Now, let's put two and two together . . . we know that neither of *us* did it—"

"I should hope not!"

"And we know Albert didn't do it—"

"Of course he didn't!"

"So who does that leave? Just Susan and George. And Aunt Etta, of course, but she never left the room."

Jessie was thoughtful. "Why . . . why, you know, Gretch, that's right. It must have been either Susan or George. Who else could it be?"

"And it couldn't be George," Gretchen drove on relentlessly, "because he wasn't even in town when Bella was killed. So we're left with Susan."

"Yes . . ." said Jessie doubtfully. "Unless they're in it together, you know, Gretch."

"You mean Susan killed her mother, and then George killed Mrs. MacGregor?"

"Yes . . . yes, that's what I mean."

"Yes. How clever of you, Jessie. We don't have any proof," said Gretchen, "but you know, I'm *positive* that's it!"

On the other side of town, the two people being ac-cused of murder at that very moment by Gretchen and Jessie were sitting playing a quiet game of Go Fish. George had come over for dinner—a meal which he had prepared by himself, since Harold was in a bad mood and was acting up. There had been a scene when it came time for Harold to go to bed, but after half an hour of screamed protests, with Susan hovering anxiously over him, he had dropped off to sleep abruptly, looking like an angel with his arms wrapped around his teddy bear. Now George and Susan, exhausted, were playing the only card game that both of them knew.

"Harold's been awful lately," Susan said. "Yesterday he practically accused me of lying to the police about Dora's being here the night Mother was murdered. Do you have any aces?"

"It's been hard for him since your mother died," said George. "Dora was here, wasn't she? Go fish."

"Yes, in fact, she was, Georgie. What do you think? Do you think I killed my mother?"

"No, no, Susie. Don't get upset. It's just with these murders and everything . . . well, it's an uneasy feeling, isn't it? *Somebody* we know did it. Do you have any fours?"

"Go fish," said Susan unsympathetically. "How do they know that? Maybe it was somebody from the outside. A crazy person. Why don't they ever consider that? Here."

There was an exchange of cards.

"Susan, honestly. It was somebody at that party. You know it was. Do you have any kings?"

"No, Georgie. Go fish."

George fished.

"I think I'm doing pretty well here," said Susan a little while later. "Do you have any sevens?"

"Go fish," said George, eyeing her cards. "You *are* doing well. Any jacks?"

"Go fish. You know, sometimes I worry about us, Georgie. Why can't we learn any more sophisticated card games? Do you know any other adults who still play Go

Fish? Why can't we learn bridge or poker or blackjack or something? I learned this game when I was five."

"Here's a jack," said George in triumph. "Look out, Susie. Do you have any eights?"

Susan looked disgruntled and handed them over.

"I win," said George. "There's something about its simplicity that's appealing, don't you think? The game, I mean. What do you say, shall we play again?"

"Oh, sure. Why not?"

George won two more games, and Susan won one. She leaned back in her chair and said, "I'm exhausted, Georgie. Totally drained. Too much Go Fish gets to me, you know, like a drug. Want some coffee or something?"

"Sure."

Over coffee and cake, George said, "Listen, Susie, there's something I've been meaning to ask you. Philo Harmonia is planning a concert in Hartford next weekend, and we're going to play that new piece I've written—you know, the string quartet. It's going to be the second half of the program. Will you go with me? Albert's welcome, too, if he wants. Please, Susie. You know I wrote that piece for you."

"Oh, all right, fine. I'll ask Albert if he's busy."

George's face broke into a big smile. "Good. Good. I'll get you free tickets."

Susan did not say anything, but she wondered how they had the audacity to charge the viewing public for tickets. Philo Harmonia was not, after all, the New York Philharmonic. She looked at George, who was humming to himself and happily dripping coffee all over his shirt. The shirt was so old and wrinkled that somehow it didn't seem to matter. Susan sighed. Was she doing the right thing? After all, she already had a son. George needed somebody to look after him almost as badly as Harold did.

It wasn't as if Harold actually *liked* him or anything. Of course, Harold always hated any man she brought home for his inspection. Nobody was good enough. George was the best of what, she admitted to herself in retrospect, had been a sorry lot.

Unbidden, the thought came to her, *But I don't have to marry anyone now . . . I'm rich . . . I don't have to do anything I don't want to do. . . .*

She was horrified at herself. What was she going to do, toss poor George on the scrap heap just because she had come into some money?

Inside, however, the voice whispered, *It's not just some money . . . it's sixty-four million dollars . . . sixty-four million dollars. . . .*

Somehow she had never thought seriously of what that meant. It meant she didn't have to work anymore . . . that she could travel, do as she pleased, see whomever she wanted, whenever she wanted. She looked doubtfully at George, as if seeing him for the first time. Was he really the man she wanted to be tied to for the rest of her life? Hadn't things somehow . . . well, *changed* between the two of them since her mother had died?

George apparently didn't think so. He sat there, unconcerned, looking just the same as always: artistic and unkempt. He was humming the third movement of Schubert's Trout Quintet. Susan turned away, suddenly annoyed. She was tired of the Trout Quintet. She was tired of ironing George's shirts for him and interceding between him and her son. She was tired of Philo Harmonia and his poorly composed pieces with their interminable viola solos. She was tired, in the final analysis, of George.

But when she looked at him again she relented. He

was a very sweet man. . . . She didn't want to make a mistake. She would think it over for a bit.

She smiled at him. "More coffee, dear?"

Gretchen was sitting in her office at school, marking essay papers. She was scowling and mumbling, "No, no, *no* . . ." as she wrote out comments in her large, bold handwriting. She was writing savagely on one student's essay, "Just because Chaucer used creative spelling doesn't mean *you* can," when Albert came into her office and sat down.

She gazed at him with concern. He was looking very tired and drained recently. Of course it was no wonder, with everything that was going on, but still . . .

"Are you all right, Albert?"

He nodded vaguely.

"Are we still going out to dinner tonight, or would you rather cancel it?"

"What? Oh, no, no . . . I mean yes, of course we're going out. We always go out on Fridays, don't we?"

"All right, then. I'll come by your office around five."

That evening, at the Golden Eagle, Albert leaned across the table, knocking over the salt and pepper shakers and a basket of bread. He did not seem to notice. He took her hand and said, "Gretchen, will you marry me?"

She was busy cleaning up the mess he had made. "Oh, Albert, *please*. Look at what you've done here."

"Gretchen. Will you marry me?"

She gazed at him, startled. "Albert—"

"Life is short, Gretch. Life is short. You never know when it's going to end." His face had a sad, haunted look. "I'll turn forty this year. I don't want to go on like this. It's not for me." He added with that strange dignity of his, "I care for you very much, Gretch. Please marry me."

"Albert—"

"We could get married this summer. In June, perhaps. June is a good time for a wedding. I'd like to get married sooner, but we can't, not with—well, you know . . ."

"These murders," she said dryly.

"Yes. These murders." He paused and leaned forward. "You don't have any idea, do you, Gretch—I mean, who might be behind all of it?"

"No. No, of course not."

"Neither do I. It seems as though if I could just *think* about it . . . just think about it the right way, the answer must be obvious, you know. Obvious. But I can't seem to see it that way at all—"

"A June wedding," Gretchen said.

"Oh. Yes. A June wedding. What do you say?"

"Yes, Albert. I say yes."

He was so gratified he knocked over his wine glass. After they had finished dinner, they went out to The Painted Man to celebrate.

"You mean it, Gretch? Really? You and Albert are getting married?" Jessie's face was flushed a mottled pink color.

"Yes, Jessie. He asked me tonight at dinner. Can you believe it? After all these years!"

"Oh—oh, Gretch . . . I'm *so* happy for both of you, I really am. This is what I've wanted for years . . . for years, Gretch. Oh, I'm so excited—and a June wedding! Oh, it's wonderful—*wonderful*!"

And she burst into tears.

"It's nothing," she said, struggling to smile as Gretchen

leaned over her worriedly. "It's just that I never . . . I never realized—oh, I'll miss you so *much*, Gretchen!"

Gretchen, very sensibly, poured her out some brandy. After a few sips Jessie perked up again and began to plan.

"You'll get married on the Whitaker estate, of course. They have the most *beautiful* back yard there, and in June it'll be all roses and those bunchy things, what are they called, not chrysanthemums . . . oh, well. I think the color of the wedding should be pink, don't you? I'll wear a deep pink, sort of a rose color, and your other bridesmaids can wear pale pink, like rosebuds. It'll be *so* romantic, Gretchen! You'll be all in white with a bouquet of sweetheart roses, I know just the place to order them from, they do it up right with lace and everything. And Albert will wear a tuxedo, of course, and the table linens can be all pastels, pink and blue and pale yellow, I think that would be *so* pretty, don't you? Let me see, I saw an illustration in a magazine the other day that would be just what I'm talking about. . . ."

And she bustled off happily to root, swinelike, in the pile of newspapers and magazines under the coffee table in the living room.

Gretchen, watching her go, smiled to herself. Dear Jessie!

The next evening, Saturday, a cheerful group bundled into George's car for the trip to the concert in Hartford.

Susan had asked Albert to come along ("Honestly, Albert, you know Georgie, he'd be so hurt if you didn't come"), and Albert in turn had corralled Gretchen and Jessie. Susan sat in the front, next to George, and the three others were crammed together in the back of the old rickety Ford. George drove a faded red Ford that, like so

many things about George, had seen better days. It rico-
cheted and backfired and made strange clackety sounds as
they drove along. Jessie, in the back seat, was convinced
she was about to die.

"Oh, be careful!" she sang out as George swung into
the left-hand lane. "Be careful! George, be *careful*! Look
over there—oh! Oh, *no*!"

"Just keep your eyes closed," Susan advised. "It's best
when George drives. The man is a maniac."

They sat through the concert, in a rented hall in Hartford, in a state somewhere between boredom and stupor.
Jessie fell asleep quite peacefully on Gretchen's shoulder.
The string quartet which George had composed was an
hour long and included, perhaps not surprisingly, five
viola solos. George had a nervous habit of humming as he
played; humming that could be heard very clearly in the
audience. Susan rolled her eyes at Albert and whispered,
"I've told him, but he never listens."

"The middle section was very nice," her brother whispered back.

"Thank you, Albert. Thank you for being kind."

Afterwards they went out for a late dinner, where they
all drank to Gretchen and Albert's engagement. Jessie
showed Albert some pictures she had of different styles of
tuxedos. Albert said to his sister, "Perhaps we'll have a
double wedding." Susan smiled nervously. A short while
later she stood up and said, "It's time for me to get back, if
you don't mind. Dora says there'll be hell to pay if she's
not home by twelve to watch *Star Trek* with Phil."

A few days later, George was driving Susan home from
work. It had been a long day at the *Ridgewood Star* and
Susan was in a bad mood. She usually worked at home,

not in the office, but she had come in to do some last-minute corrections on one of her "What's New in Ridgewood" columns. "The problem is," she was saying furiously to George, "that nothing is new in Ridgewood. Nothing ever is new in Ridgewood. My mother's death and Mrs. MacGregor's death were the biggest things to happen around here in years. I refused to write about them—well, at least the idiots in the editorial office can understand that—so what's left? How many people were at the skating rink last weekend? That's not news. It's not *news*, Georgie."

George nodded sympathetically, cut off another car with a squealing of brakes and mutual insults, and careened along in the left-hand lane.

"And then when I went out to lunch," Susan continued hotly, "I ran into that self-righteous prig Lizzie Feldencraft, who told me she had read my last child-care column and thought it was the stupidest thing she had ever heard. She said all her children had been allowed to cry themselves to sleep alone at night, and look how they turned out. I agreed with her. I said, 'That's right, look how they turned out.' Well, she didn't like that at all, George. I told her it was just plain cruel to let a child cry itself to sleep all alone, no matter what the so-called experts say, and that my Harold had never been allowed to do that. Even when he's upset, I'm there for him. So then, naturally, you can *imagine* what she said . . ."

After an exchange of mutual insults concerning their offspring, the two mothers had retreated to opposite sides of the Golden Eagle lunchroom and glared at each other throughout the meal. "Self-righteous prig," Susan said now. "Bitch! Conceited bitch! Why, if I *told* you the things she said to me—"

George nodded again, cut back into the middle lane, passed a car on the right and stopped at a traffic light with a loud protesting squeal of brakes. Susan lurched forward. Something bright and shiny rolled out from under her seat.

"George?" She picked it up. "What . . . what's this?"

In her palm was a diamond-and-sapphire earring in the graceful shape of a flower.

George's mouth formed a comical "O" of surprise as he stared, astonished, at the earring. "What—?" he spluttered. *"Where—?"*

The car behind them honked, and George put his foot on the accelerator. He turned off onto a side street and parked. Then he said feebly, "Where did it come from?"

"Here, Georgie. Under the seat."

They stared at each other in silence.

"Is it—?"

"Yes. It's my mother's earring."

George had gone very pale. "It's—it's horrible. . . . Somebody's trying to frame me!"

"Who's been in this car, Georgie?"

"Nobody. Nobody—just you and Albert and Gretchen and Jessie . . ." His hands were shaking. "That concert the other night," he whispered.

"That's right." Susan thought back. The three of them had been in the back seat. "What are we going to do?"

George stared at her, wide-eyed. "What do you mean? What do you mean? We have to take it to the police. What else can we do?"

"We could throw it away, or hide it somewhere else."

"Susan!"

"I don't want Albert implicated," she said fiercely. "You understand me, George? I don't want Albert implicated in this."

"Albert?" George shrieked. He bounced up and his head hit the ceiling. "Albert? How about *me*? Can you

spare a thought for me, Susan? I'll be the first person the police will think of! It was in *my car*, for God's sake!"

"That's true, George. That's true. It does look bad for you."

He rested his head miserably on the steering wheel. "I'm not an idiot, Susie, no matter what anybody thinks. I wouldn't plant the damned earring on myself and leave it for somebody to find. I swear to you, I've never seen the damned thing before. I've never seen it before!"

"Yes . . . I know, Georgie. I know. But who . . . ?"

They stared at each other.

George said in a whisper, *"One of the three people who were in the back seat that night . . ."*

6

Detective Janovy said, "Are you sure this is the earring that your mother was wearing, Miss Whitaker?"

"Yes, Detective. I'm sure."

"You have the match to it?"

"Yes. It's in a safe-deposit box at our bank. I'll ask Albert to get it tomorrow, if you like."

"Thank you."

Janovy, Susan, and George were sitting on the two shabby sofas in George's ramshackle apartment. Susan and George had driven straight there after their discovery and called the police.

"So it was underneath the seat of the car?"

"Yes."

Janovy regarded George Drexler thoughtfully. *Why?* he thought. Why had someone placed it there? Why, in fact, had the killer kept it in the first place?

George was looking very much the worse for wear. He looked downtrodden and depressed. He had his viola out and was plucking at the string dispiritedly, a soft pizzicato emphasis to his words. "Somebody hates me," he said sadly. "Somebody hates me."

"Oh, *Georgie.*"

"It's true, Susan. Somebody hates me. Is it something about me? What have I ever done to deserve this? Someone needed a stooge, and they picked me. It's so *unfair.*"

"Cheer up, George. Would you like something hot to drink? Wouldn't that be soothing?"

George perked up a little bit. "Yes, thanks, that would be great. Hold on a sec, I'll make it. Yes, you stay right here. Anything for you, Detective?"

"No, thanks."

"What would you like, Susie? Tea or coffee?"

"Tea, please."

"Caffeinated or decaffeinated or herbal?"

"Caffeinated is fine."

"Good. I have Twinings Earl Grey, English Breakfast, Assam, Queen Mary—that's really special—Darjeeling, Irish Breakfast, and Prince of Wales."

"It doesn't really matter, George. Whatever."

He vanished into the kitchen. Susan turned to Detective Janovy. "I hope you don't mind, but I wanted to get George out of the room for a minute. I'd like to know what you're thinking, Detective."

"What do you mean?"

"Well . . ." She glanced at him a trifle uncomfortably. "I hope you don't suspect my brother. I know Albert. I'm telling you, nobody in our family is a murderer."

A strange echo of one of the first things Albert had ever said to him, thought Janovy. *We're not murderers,* Albert had said. *You don't know us, that's all. You'll see when you meet my sister. It's not the way it looks.*

At the time Janovy had thought, *I'll be the judge of that,* and he still felt that way. Nobody told him how to think, especially not during a murder investigation. He said, "I understand how you feel, Miss Whitaker, but I haven't ruled anyone out yet. It's my job to keep an open mind."

"Yes, of course. It's just that . . . well, it does seem awfully *odd* that the earring would be found in George's car, doesn't it? I mean, why would somebody do that?"

There are lots of reasons, thought Janovy. He was puzzled and suspicious. Surely this was an odd tack for her to take?

"I don't know," he replied stiffly. "But I intend to find out."

At that point George bustled back into the room with a black lacquered Japanese tray in his hands. On it were two large steaming mugs. They were of different designs—one

had a picture of a house on it, while the other said *La Vache* and sported a picture of a solemn-looking cow. They were both chipped around the edges, but George did not seem to notice. He handed Susan her cup and said, "Prince of Wales tea, plenty of milk, no sugar, madam."

"Thank you, George."

Janovy got to his feet. "I'll be on my way," he said. "May I use your phone, Mr. Drexler? I'd like to call ahead and see if Dr. Schneider and Miss Lowell are at home."

"I've never seen it before in my life," Gretchen said firmly. "How about you, Jessie?"

"Oh, no . . . no, certainly not—"

"Neither of us has ever seen it before, Detective. Does that answer your question? May I ask where you found it?"

"In George Drexler's car."

Jessie let out a little yip of surprise. Gretchen merely raised an eyebrow. "I see," she said. "So anyone who's been in that car since the murder—"

"—may have planted it there. That's right."

Jessie was looking very flustered, he thought. She cast nervous glances at her friend. Gretchen was calm and composed, as always. She sat with her hands folded in her lap. There was a short silence, then she said, "I agree that it looks bad, Detective, since we were in that car only a few days ago, and now the earring is found. I can only assure you that neither Jessie nor I had anything to do with it. Albert had described what it looked like to me, of course, but I've certainly never seen it before. Although it's not hard to recognize it as one of Mrs. Whitaker's things. Showy, as usual."

She said it with disapproval.

He remained a short while longer, but there was no more information forthcoming from the two women. They both maintained that they had never seen the earring before. They said so in very emphatic terms. And they assured him that Albert Whitaker had not seen it since his mother's death, either.

"To put it on the floor like that," said Gretchen with disdain, "is such . . . such a *sly* thing to do. Don't you agree, Jessie?"

"Oh, yes, Gretchen. Of course I do. Sly is the very word."

"We may have our faults, but neither one of us is sly, Detective. You can see that for yourself. To do that—well, it's just so *underhanded*, if you know what I mean."

"Yes. I do."

"Poor George. How is he taking it?"

"Not very well, I'm afraid," said Janovy, remembering the unhappy pizzicato.

"I must give him a call," she said, and rose to her feet. She waited until he rose also. "Thank you so much for dropping by," she said, as if it had been a social call from an old friend. "And the very best of luck, Detective."

Albert, like everyone else, denied stoutly that he had seen the earring since his mother died.

"Of course I recognize it," he said in his soft reasonable voice. "Of course I recognize it. My mother used to wear those earrings all the time. Well, not *all* the time, actually, just for special occasions, but you see what I mean."

"Yes, Dr. Whitaker. But since her death—"

"I certainly didn't take it and plant it on George. Why would I do that? What do I have against poor old George?

And if you're going to say that I was just trying to get rid of it, well, that's ridiculous. I could simply throw it away, assuming, of course, that I was the one who had it, which isn't the case. You see?"

Janovy, unfortunately, did see. The next day, he accompanied Albert to the bank and waited while Albert conferred with the bank manager. They were led to the safe-deposit box and it was unlocked, with great ceremony. The two earrings matched exactly.

"There," said Albert. "I told you it was hers. The question is, who planted it on George?"

While good at identifying the vital question, Albert claimed he had no answers. He had not seen Gretchen or Jessie drop anything on the car floor.

"It's impossible, absolutely impossible. You don't understand, Detective. None of them would do it. Kill my mother, I mean. You don't know them—Gretchen or Jessie or my sister. You simply don't understand."

"Perhaps not," said Janovy briefly. He shook hands and took his leave.

"So the earring has turned up," said Philip West. "The question is, what does it mean?"

"I don't know, sir," said Janovy. "The thing is, George Drexler is the only one of that group who has a valid alibi. He was nowhere around here when Mrs. Whitaker was killed. I wonder . . ."

"What, Paul?"

"Nothing. I just wonder if someone is trying to implicate him anyway. Maybe the murderer feels the need for more concealment."

"If that's true, that means you're getting somewhere. You've been digging and digging, and somebody might be getting nervous. Perhaps they didn't expect the investigation to go on this long—"

"Or maybe they didn't expect to have to kill Mrs. MacGregor in order to silence her," said Janovy. "The killer counted on just one death, and now there's two. That could be making someone nervous."

"Yes. Well, it sounds like things are beginning to shake up a bit. You've got it down to the group in that car. Think Susan Whitaker would plant the earring on her own fiancé, if she felt he was getting off scot-free—or maybe to protect somebody else?"

Janovy flushed. It was hard to believe. His impression of Susan Whitaker had been so favorable. But still . . . "Yes. It's possible. She's very concerned that I not suspect her brother, and her brother's the same way about her."

"Hmmmph. That's interesting. Well, it's coming along, Paul. It's coming along. I told you there was no such thing as a perfect murder."

"I hope not," said Janovy earnestly.

Snooky took a sip of the hot drink and said, "Hot cider, rum, cinnamon, nutmeg, a little orange juice, buckwheat honey, some brandy and—" he took another sip—"cloves."

"Very good, Snookers," said his sister.

"I don't understand," Bernard said. "How did he learn to do that?"

"He didn't learn, Bernard. It's an inborn talent. A gift. My mother used to say he could analyze his bottle formula."

Bernard looked sulky. "That was my secret recipe for a hot toddy. Now it's out. He could tell people about it if he wanted to."

"Grow up, Bernard. That's one thing about my little

talents, none of them are worth much. How about trying something else? Make it hard this time."

While Bernard turned his back and mixed another drink, Snooky continued, "And I have some news. I just spoke to Susan. It's about the missing earring. Apparently it's been found."

He related this briefly.

"I see."

"Do you, Bernard?"

"Yes."

"What is it that you see?"

"More than you can ever imagine," said Bernard firmly. "That earring was part of a set that Bella was wearing that night, wasn't it?"

"Yes. I've seen her wear it before. Fabulous stuff. Diamonds and sapphires. Susan told me her father gave it to her mother years and years ago. I can't imagine what it's worth now. I'll say one thing about Bella, she could dress up like nobody's business. If she had gone out that night she would have swept into the restaurant and everybody's mouth would have been hanging open. The maître d' would have let her mop the floor with him if she wanted to. She had that kind of style."

"How fascinating," said Bernard. He lifted up the bottle of Tabasco sauce and looked at it thoughtfully. "Where's the matching earring?"

"The other one? In a safety deposit box at the bank. Susan told me she and Albert put it away with the rest of the set."

"Are you sure of that?"

"Certainly I'm sure." Snooky gave him an uneasy glance. "Why, you don't think that—"

"I don't think anything. Here, Snooky. Try this drink. It's got a magic ingredient. I've got him now, Maya. If he guesses this right, I'll—I'll drink this bottle of Tabasco sauce."

"Don't say that, sweetheart. I've never known him to make a mistake."

Snooky took a sip and grimaced. "Good Lord, Bernard, you don't have to *poison* me, do you? Let's see now . . . it's tomato juice, a dash of Tabasco, garlic, cloves again—ugh, what a combination—whisky, and a touch of some other spice, let's see, I think it's cardamom. Am I right?"

Bernard was looking pleased. "Not quite."

"There's something else?"

"Yes."

Snooky took another sip, choked and said, "I give up. What is it?"

"Dog food."

Maya let out a faint shriek of laughter.

A little while later Bernard went up to his study, closed the door, put a page in the typewriter and, after turning the light out and plunging the room into pitch darkness, began to type.

Mr. Whiskers had finally become more cooperative. He was still obsessed with his own reflection, but he had left the mirror long enough to get involved in a series of swashbuckling adventures, and in a romance with a young pink-eyed mouse from the neighboring village. Bernard wasn't too sure whether it was possible for rats and mice to interbreed, but he figured, rather sensibly, that this was a question that would probably not occupy the minds of his four- to six-year-old readers.

He worked for a while in the darkened room, typing

along madly as Mr. Whiskers attacked a baker's boy and made off with the bread he carried. He took the bread to the home of his beloved and they had a feast. She fluttered her long pale eyelashes and sighed, "Now if we only had some cheese," and Mr. Whiskers was out the door like a shot, heading toward the cheese shop in town. "Now if we only had some lettuce for a salad," she said when he brought back half a wheel of soft blue triple-crème cheese. Mr. Whiskers headed off, a little more grudgingly this time. The lady mouse was up to, "Now if we only had golden goblets to drink the wine out of," when Bernard decided she would have to go.

"Avaricious little bitch," he said, and pulled the page from the typewriter. He sat despondently in the darkness, mourning Mr. Whiskers's bad taste in women, then switched on his desk lamp and took out his notebook. He uncapped the green Magic Marker, sat thoughtfully for a while and then wrote:

ERRNG

"Earring," he said, and grunted.

Misty scratched at the door and he let her in. She looked at him, gauging his readiness for a walk outdoors, then yawned and settled down under the desk at his feet.

Bernard wrote:

GRGS CR

"George's car," he said out loud. Then:

SHFT SSPCN
PLNT LSWHR
Y KP T N FRST PLC?

These, when deciphered, meant *shift suspicion; plant elsewhere,* and *why keep it in first place?* Bernard sat and looked at his notes for a long time. The page with Mr. Whiskers's aborted relationship lay forgotten on the floor. Finally Bernard put away his notebook and sighed. Much as he hated the thought of actually coming into contact with anybody outside his house, there were a few questions he felt he had to ask. . . .

Etta Pinsky went into the tiny kitchen of her apartment and took the whistling kettle off the heat. She took out an old, chipped blue teacup and saucer, put a tea bag in it, and poured the water in. She carefully added three spoonfuls of sugar and then, with a sigh, sat down at the rickety kitchen table, which was simply a folding card table with two chairs around it.

Etta looked around at the kitchen, with its fading flowered wallpaper and its old stove and fridge. Her things. All her old things. Her husband Vinnie had left her comfortably off, but she didn't like to buy anything new, preferring instead to be surrounded by her old familiar things. She liked to watch them age along with her. No use buying a lot of new stuff, she thought philosophically. She was eighty years old now. New furniture would just make her feel older. This way she could look at the wallpaper and remember when she bought it, forty years ago, and the terrible fuss that Vinnie had kicked up because it was so expensive. *Expensive!* she thought. It wouldn't be expensive by today's standards. Of course everything was worth more in the old days. The dollar was worth something then. *She* was worth something then. Now she was old and worn-out, just like her wallpaper.

She thoughtfully rubbed a burnt spot on the top of the

table and remembered how Vinnie's old friend Max had dropped a match there one night during a poker game. Max had been lighting his cigar, puffing furiously and in between puffs shouting at Ralph, who had just bluffed him out of twenty-three dollars with nothing but a pair of fours in his hand. "You shlemiel! You goddamned shlemiel!" Max had shouted, and had dropped the match, nearly sending the card table and the players up in flames. Ever since then, whenever Max got upset the other men would silently point to the burnt spot. Poor Max, thought Etta. How he loved to get angry. How he loved it when his oldest friend Ralph would bluff him and win. Max had died twenty years ago. Ralph had died shortly afterwards.

Etta sighed and her eyes roamed around the room. So many memories . . . her gaze rested thoughtfully on the corner next to the fridge, where a heap of fuzz balls and dust remained, despite MacGregor's halfhearted attempts at cleaning. Harriet MacGregor, thought Etta. Another old friend who was gone. She felt very old and dusty and gray herself, all of a sudden. Really, perhaps it would be best to have a little cry, all to herself.

She pushed away the teacup, which rattled on its saucer, and put her head slowly down on the table.

She was still sitting there a little while later when the doorbell rang. Goodness, she thought, I *am* getting old. She had completely forgotten that Snooky and that likable brother-in-law of his, what's his name, Bernard Something, were coming over for tea. Snooky had called earlier and asked if they could drop by.

"Bernard wants to talk to you," he had said. "This is a banner day. You don't know it, but Bernard never wants to talk to *anyone*."

Come at four, she had said, and then with her thoughts of the past, she had forgotten. Luckily there was tea, and plenty of cake left over from yesterday. She got up slowly and went to the door.

She showed them into the living room, and went back into the kitchen to make more tea. Bernard looked around. The furniture was old and hard and had that indefinable musty smell of furniture which has stood in the same place for decades and never been moved. It was good solid furniture, made of walnut, and it gave a sense of importance and weight to the room. The windows were narrow and there was not much light, but Bernard felt comfortable with that. "Nice room."

"I knew you'd like it," said Snooky.

"Go help her with whatever she's doing in there, Snooky. Unless you enjoy letting an eighty-year-old woman wait on you."

Snooky came back a few minutes later with a tea tray. Etta poured out for the three of them and cut them each a large slice of pound cake. Then she leaned back on the divan and said sharply, "Why are you here?"

"We came by to see you," said Snooky.

"Come on, Snooky. I'm not that old yet. I haven't had two young men who weren't even related to me drop by this place in more than forty years. Why are you here?"

"I came to ask you about your niece's murder," said Bernard.

Etta looked at him curiously and nodded.

"I wondered whether you could repeat to me what Mrs. MacGregor said to you before she died."

"You mean what she told me here, when she was hinting around about something?"

"Yes."

The old woman sipped her tea, her eyes vacant. "Har-

riet MacGregor loved to have secrets. She loved to know
something before everyone else did. It got her killed in
the end, didn't it? Let me see. She was starting to sweep
up in the kitchen—not that that made much of a difference to the kitchen floor, let me tell you—and she was
giggling to herself the way she always did when she had
something to tell me. Well, I wasn't going to put up with
it, so I asked her what was so funny. She wouldn't tell me.
Then she started to work, if you can call it that, and even
when I pointed out some spots she had missed, she didn't
mind. That wasn't like her. No, it wasn't like her at all.
Usually she got upset at the least little thing I said. But
that day she just giggled some more. I could see that there
would be no work done until she had spilled the beans, so
I gave her a cup of tea and we sat down to talk. We often
did talk while she worked," Etta added. "I realize now
that I hired her more for the company than anything else.
Anyway, one or the other of us brought up that black mink
coat that Albert had given her. MacGregor was terribly
excited about it. I don't think she had ever owned anything like it in her life. She said it was beautiful, and then
it seemed to remind her of something, because she said
there was something else—something else that had happened the night that Bella was killed. . . ."

"Miss Pinsky—"

"Call me Aunt Etta. Everyone does."

"Aunt Etta, can you remember the words she used?
Can you tell me what she said, *exactly*?"

Etta screwed up her face into a tight knot and closed
her eyes. "I'm not sure . . . it was something like, 'The
coat is so beautiful. And there's something else . . . something else it brought to mind that I should tell you.' Then
she said something about that detective not being as smart
as he made himself out to be. She was still all fussed up

over his asking whether she had left by the back door. She had her pride, Mrs. MacGregor did."

"He asked her how she left the house?"

"Yes, and naturally she was all insulted. That was the way she was. So she said something about him not being so smart, and that if he knew what *she* knew . . ."

"So she knew something because she left by the front door," said Bernard. "Is it possible—do you think she saw who was hiding in the hallway?"

Etta pondered this, then shook her head. "That wasn't the impression I got. I don't think she was talking about a person. It seemed to me she was talking about some*thing*, not someone . . . as if there was something she saw or knew about that the detective had overlooked. She loved knowing things that other people didn't," she added tartly. "And when I tried to get her to tell me about it, she just shut her mouth and wouldn't say anything except that *it didn't make any sense.* She would have figured it out eventually and maybe told me, but unfortunately she didn't get to live that long."

"*It didn't make any sense,*" muttered Bernard.

"Yes. I told her that nothing she said ever made much sense. More tea, either of you?"

"No, thanks," said Snooky. Bernard did not reply. His eyes were curiously blank.

"Bernard's gone into one of his comas," said Snooky. "Embarrassing, I always find it. He doesn't seem to mind. Of course, he's never very social at the best of times."

"I was just thinking hard," Bernard said. "Naturally you wouldn't recognize what that looked like, Snooky. Thank you very much, Aunt Etta. You've been very helpful."

She gave him a shrewd glance. "Thinking you'll get to

it quicker than the police, are you? I wouldn't count on it."

"No . . . no, I suppose not."

She and Snooky chatted for a while. Bernard had lapsed into another one of his reveries, staring out the window with a glazed look in his eyes.

"Narcolepsy," Snooky said. "Sad, isn't it? If you don't mind, Aunt Etta, I'll just drag him out by his feet to the car, and we'll be on our way."

They said good-bye to Aunt Etta, who accompanied them to the front entrance of the apartment house and watched them as they left.

"Letter for you," said Maya.

Snooky looked up apprehensively. "It's not another one from Deirdre, is it?"

"Guess again, Snooks. This one is from William."

"Take it away and burn it, please."

Maya held it out wordlessly. Snooky ripped the envelope open and, after steeling himself with a large gulp of coffee, read through the letter with a stony expression on his face. Then he picked up the newspaper and went back to doing the crossword puzzle.

Maya said, "A bad one this time, Snooks?"

"Not too bad."

"Mind if I read it?"

"Help yourself."

Maya picked up the letter. It was typed on William's word processor, on thick cream-colored stationery with the initials WSR across the top in a dark blue diamond design. Maya could not remember the last time she had received a letter actually handwritten by William himself. Except for short notes to members of his own family,

William went straight to his word processor. The only time she had ever seen him use his gold fountain pen was to punch out the numbers on his pocket calculator.

> Dear Snooky *(the letter began),*
> How are you? Emily and I and the children are well. We had a great time in Honolulu last month. I hope you are enjoying your visit at Maya's. Please remember that her home is not your home. But I did not write to hector you, as you have accused me of doing in the past. I have been thinking lately about your inheritance. I suppose it will come as no surprise to you that I feel *very strongly* that you should put at least some of it aside as an investment. I don't know where you are keeping your money these days, probably stuffed into a burlap bag and hidden under your mattress, but I feel I can help you maximize your returns. Treasury bills are a secure way to invest your money; also, I know of some tax-free bonds that you might be interested in. Give Maya and Bernard my love, and I look forward to hearing from you soon.
>
> Your loving brother,
> William

Underneath, Emily had scribbled,

> P.S. Snooky, you should listen to your brother, he worries about you all the time, and he only wants what's best.

"It's pathetic," Maya said. "Simply pathetic. They never stop trying, do they?"

"What I can't understand is, why does he always sign it 'Your brother'? Does he think I don't know who he is by now?"

"Where *is* your money, by the way, Snooks?"

"Oh, you know, Maya. Here and there. Here and there." He waved a hand in the air. "I get interest checks from time to time, from around the country. It doesn't bother me. I get by."

Maya regarded him fondly. Snooky indeed did get by. When he was not encroaching on someone else's hospitality, he would rent a house for himself. He would stay in one place for a while, then move on when the impulse struck.

"No stability," William would say in funereal tones. "No security. Not like you and me, Maya. Not like you and me."

"Snooky doesn't value security, William. He likes change."

William would make a forlorn mooing sound. "*Change!* Change? Who honestly likes change? Nobody! A lonely old age, that's what he's building for himself. Mark my words, Maya. A poverty-stricken old age."

"William, honestly. Snooky is only twenty-five years old."

"A poverty-stricken old age," her older brother would say with relish. "I only hope I'm here to see it, Maya. I just pray I'm here to see it."

Now Maya said worriedly, "I hate to tell you this, Snooks, but I think that William has a point. Maybe you should invest some of your money with him. No matter what else you can say about him, he's a good businessman. You could at least consider it."

"I have considered it, Maya. I've been considering it while I've been trying to think what fourteen down, a wealthy person, nine letters, ends in S, could be. And I've decided to nip this whole idea in the bud. Do you mind if I call William from here?"

"All right. Go ahead."

Snooky went to the kitchen phone and dialed rapidly. "Hello? Hello, who is this? Anna?" Anna was William's six-year-old daughter. "Hello, Anna, how are you? This is your Uncle Snooky calling. Can I speak to your daddy, please? What? No, Anna . . . what? Anna, I don't want to talk to your doll first. Anna . . . listen to me, you little . . . oh, all right. All right." In a resigned tone he said, "Hello, dolly. What? That's not her name? Well, what's her name? Emily? You can't name her Emily, honey, that's your mommy's name. What? You know? All right. Hello, Emily. How are you today? Now, can I speak to your daddy, please, Anna? Good. Good. Yes, I'll talk to your doll while you go find him. Hello, dolly, how's the stock market these days?" Snooky covered the mouthpiece and said in a hoarse whisper, "She has a doll named Emily. Isn't that a little strange? Does that seem Freudian to you? Do you think she sticks pins in it or something? Hello?" he said into the phone. "William? Snooky here. Yes. Yes, an adorable little minx, yes. Listen, William, down to business. I got your letter." Pause. "Treasury bills? Maybe. What do I mean, maybe? Well, to tell you the truth, William, I have something—well, something a little awkward to tell you. Maybe you'd better sit down. You're not going to like it much. You see, William—I hope this doesn't upset you, I really do—well, you see, I've already spent all the money you gave me. Yes. That's right. All of my inheritance. I'm afraid so. Oh, about a year ago. That's right, it only lasted about two or three years. I want to tell you how truly sorry I am, William. I know what a disappointment it is to you, with your business sense and all. It was a lot of fun while it lasted, though. So you see, I'm afraid your investment advice is a little . . . well, it's a little too late for that. Thanks anyway. How's Emily? And Buster?" Buster was William's ten-year-old son. "Good. Good. Fine. Talk to you soon. Okay. I will. They say hello, too. Bye."

Maya had listened to all this curiously, sipping her coffee. Snooky came back to the dining room table and sat down. He picked up the paper and murmured.

"Wealthy person, nine letters . . . hmmmmm . . ."

"Snooks?"

"Hmmm?"

"How'd he take it?"

"William? Oh, he took it fine. He knew I was just putting him on. One thing I have to say about William, I've never been able to put one over on him."

"He got the message, though?"

"Uh-huh. I think he'll back off for a while. Is there any more coffee, Maya?"

As she handed him the coffee pot, Snooky exclaimed in triumph, *"Moneybags,"* and filled it in neatly.

Jessie Lowell, as she did every year, was helping out with the local rummage sale. This was a big event in Ridgewood; a hall was rented in the center of town, near the art gallery, and for two weeks ahead of time people came by and donated old, used objects and clothing. All the proceeds went to charity. Jessie had volunteered for ten years running and was, by now, one of the leading lights of the Ridgewood Rummage Sale. During the weeks of preparation, her personality changed completely. Ordinarily so shy, hesitant, and unsure of herself, she changed overnight into a dominating shrew, bossing around her underlings and fussily rearranging the sale items. Every year Gretchen regarded this change in her friend with bemusement. Jessie even became more authoritative at home, instructing Gretchen how to make proper broiled chicken ("I always baste it *first*, and rub it with butter, not margarine, Gretch"), and eating far more than her fair share. She even complained about how untidy the house was, and went around straightening things and mumbling to herself. This year Gretchen had decided to simply stay out of Jessie's way until the whole thing was over.

Now Jessie was fussing over one of the tables, making sure that everything was arranged to her own satisfaction, if not that of the teenage girl who was in charge of the table.

"Now, now, Henrietta," she was saying, "this pair of pants doesn't go here, it should go over *here*, next to this pretty sweater; you see what a nice combination that makes?"

Henrietta, a pale blonde girl with a willowy figure and a decided squint, was polishing her nails. She looked bored and nodded.

"And this nice wool skirt, what a lovely English heather that is, should go over here, next to this silk blouse that Mrs. Rivera donated. Don't you agree, Henrietta?"

"Sure, why not," said Henrietta. She held up one hand and blew on her fingernails vigorously.

"Be careful of that nail polish, dear, you're going to spill it all over the clothes." Jessie picked up the bottle of polish and surveyed it critically. "You know, Henrietta dear, you really shouldn't wear such a bright red. It looks positively *slutty*, it really does."

This was the kind of remark that Jessie would normally never dream of making. Henrietta merely shrugged.

"Anyway, dear, I'll be off now. Don't you rearrange anything, I think it's perfect now. Bye-bye!"

Henrietta waved limply with the other hand. Jessie bustled off, saying to herself,

"I don't know *what* the young are coming to . . . what a color, positively *slutty,* my mother would have called it . . . anyway, where is that lovely piece of crockery that Mr. Henderson, bless his soul, brought in yesterday . . .?"

She pushed her mousy brown hair off her forehead and wedged her ample figure in between two tables. "Hello, Lisa," she said to the other teenage girl who had volunteered to help. "Where's that piece of crockery Mr. Henderson gave us?"

Lisa, a neurotic-looking girl with dark hair, glasses and a worried expression, pointed. "It's over there, Miss Lowell."

"Ah, yes, that's right. What else have we gotten so far today?"

Lisa, with an expression of triumph, produced a neatly labeled, alphabetized list. "Angora sweater," she read out loud. "Cotton sweater (red), piece of crockery, wooden doll, painted elephant (porcelain), three hats, one letter opener (silver), one mohair sweater, a set of napkins, four pairs of pants, and one rabbit."

"A rabbit?"

"A wooden rabbit. Over there."

Jessie's eyes followed her finger to a large, grotesquely carved white rabbit with pink ears, pink nose and painted black whiskers. One of its ears was shorter than the other and its face was lopsided, giving it a disturbed and pathetic look. "Good Lord, who gave us *that*?"

"Mr. Valpasso."

Jessie nodded. Ernest Valpasso labored under the delusion that he was an expert woodcarver. Fortunately it

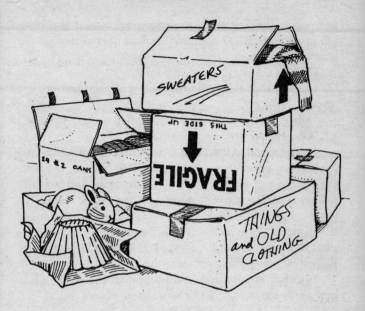

was only his hobby, and most of his time was taken up with his work as an accountant in a local law firm. At Christmastime a barrage of oddly shaped wooden objects would emerge from his workshop, to be distributed among his relatives and friends. This one must have been left over; or perhaps, thought Jessie cynically, it had been returned.

She took the list and looked it over. "Very nice work, Lisa. Very nice indeed."

Lisa smiled grimly. "Thank you, Miss Lowell."

Who was Lisa performing for, Jessie wondered idly as she handed the list back. She looked down with compassion on the girl's tight, unhappy face. Her parents? Her teachers? Oh, well, there was no way of knowing. Jessie was old enough to have had Lisa in day care, ten years ago, when she first came to Ridgewood, and it had been the same then. Lisa had started making lists as soon as she learned to write.

"Where's Albert?" Jessie said now.

Lisa looked alarmed. This was an item not on her agenda. "Albert?"

"Albert Whitaker. He was supposed to be here by now."

"Oh. He's over there, Miss Lowell."

Jessie turned. Albert and Gretchen, both of whom had been (as in previous years) coerced into helping her with the sale, were lounging about shamelessly and actually *talking*, just *talking*, instead of arranging their respective tables. Albert had a coffee cup in his hand, from the big silver percolator which squatted (immense in its own dignity) in the middle of the room, and it looked like some of the coffee was spilling out onto the clothes—!

"Albert!" she shrilled, and hurried off to deal with this new evidence of everyone else's incompetence.

Snooky and Maya were upstairs, burrowing in Bernard's closet for clothes to give to the sale.

Maya looked pensively at the mess. "You start in that corner, Snooks, and I'll start over here. If you haven't seen Bernard wearing it recently, put it in the box."

"How do I know he doesn't want it any more?"

"Snooky, come on. Bernard has only two or three outfits that he'll wear. You know how he is. Most of this stuff just sits in here year after year."

Snooky unearthed a blue-and-yellow tie. "What's wrong with this?"

"His Aunt Thelma gave it to him. It has bad associations. She used to visit him when he was little and frighten him by doing her Humpty Dumpty impersonation."

"There's a scary thought. How about this one?"

"Snooky, take a look at it. Bernard's grandmother gave it to him. She has no taste whatsoever."

"Oh. How about this one?"

"It's yours if you want it, Snooks." The tie in question sported red squares on a pale pink background. Snooky knotted it around his neck.

"Nothing wrong with it," he said. "Nothing at all."

Bernard came into the room and looked impassively at his brother-in-law. "It suits you, Snooky. It really does."

"Thank you, Bernard. Hey, how about this one?"

Once Snooky was finished scavenging, he and Maya put everything into a box, along with some of Maya's old clothes, and drove over to the rented hall. When they came in, things were in chaos. Boxes were piled up in one corner and people were standing around looking lost. It was the day before the big sale, and everyone was bringing in last-minute donations. Lisa had worked herself into a frenzy, and was frantically making out list after list, her eyes clouded with tears. Susan and George were arguing over why Susan had put six of George's shirts, ones which he insisted had hardly been worn, in an "old clothing" box. "Because, George," Susan was saying in an aggrieved tone, "*all* your clothing looks like it should be either thrown away or given away. Hello, Snooky. Listen, I have something awful to tell you. Jessie was asking for more volunteers, and I opened my mouth and your name came out. I feel terrible about it now. Do you mind?"

Snooky smiled. "No, not at all."

By the end of the evening, nearly all the boxes had been unpacked and their contents laid out neatly on the eight large tables arranged around the room in a rough circle. Jessie was checking the latest of Lisa's lists with satisfaction, the one with the names of the volunteers.

"Susan," she murmured, putting a large black X next to the name. "George. Albert. Gretchen. Snooky. Henrietta. Lisa. And me." She nodded. "That should do it." She put down the list and stood in the middle of the room, her hands on her hips, rotating slowly, surveying her domain with a critical eye. *Oh, yes,* she thought, *yes, yes, it's going to go very well . . . I can feel it . . . very well indeed . . . we have such nice things this year—*

"Jessie," called Gretchen, "Jessie, come over here. We don't know where this stuff should go."

Jessie bustled off, inflated with her own self-importance.

Half an hour later a final batch of boxes came in, along with a flurry of apologies and excuses from the owners ("The whole thing just slipped my mind, I don't know how it happened. I'm so sorry, Jessie. I know how you feel about getting things in ahead of time"). Jessie waved them away with a magisterial gesture and deigned to unpack the boxes herself. She knelt down next to the boxes with undisguised enthusiasm, her untidy brown hair falling into her face, muttering to herself, "Oh, my, look at *this* . . . that's quite nice, isn't it? We'll get a good price for that—oh, my goodness, what's this thing? . . . People are so *peculiar,* aren't they? . . . I wonder what they used *that* for. . . ."

Jessie, quite innocently, was a pryer, someone who liked to look into the crowded corners of people's lives, someone who always opened other people's medicine cabinets while a visitor in their home. She had admitted to herself years ago that part of her interest and joy in running the rummage sale was, quite frankly, voyeuristic.

Now she continued happily rummaging through the Barton family possessions. "Good grief, what's *this?*" She turned it this way and that, surveying it doubtfully. It looked like a miniature jungle gym made out of red-and-yellow toothpicks. "One of the kids' things," she concluded at last. "At least, I hope so." Dr. Barton was a dentist, but Jessie hadn't realized that toothpick sculptures were a specialty. "Oh, *my*!" The next item was a lamp shade made entirely out of tongue depressors. "Imagine *that*!"

It was somewhere between the tongue depressor lamp shade and one of the strangest ties she had ever seen, a lurid purple affair with a picture of Ronald McDonald in the middle, that Jessie took a Barbie doll out of the box and began to walk it around on the floor. The doll was tall and slender and moved with stiff, graceless, jerky movements.

A little while later Gretchen came by, on her way over to Albert's table. She cast a glance at Jessie, who was still sitting on the floor, staring in a very odd way at some kind of doll she held clenched in her hand.

"Jess? Are you all right?"

Jessie gave a little jump, as if startled. She gave Gretchen an odd, furtive, hunted look.

"Oh, yes, Gretch, I'm fine . . . just fine. . . ."

"Everything all right with the unpacking?" Gretchen asked cheerfully.

"Oh, yes. Yes, *indeed*. No problem."

"That's good."

Gretchen moved on, and Jessie was left alone in the middle of the floor. She looked at the doll again and mumbled, "It *can't* be . . . no, it *can't* be. . . ."

Finally she straightened up and said out loud, "No . . . no . . . that *can't* be right!"

"Is Bernard going to the rummage sale tomorrow?" asked Snooky.

"Don't be ridiculous," said his sister.

"What's so ridiculous about it?"

"A room filled with screaming, haggling women? Don't be stupid."

"Well, I'm going," said Snooky. "Jessie assigned me to table number four."

"That's nice. Have fun."

"You're not going either?" he asked despondently.

"No."

"Why not, My? There's some good stuff there."

"You pick it up for me if you see anything I'd like. Okay?"

"Okay."

Bernard came into the living room and sat down in his favorite overstuffed armchair by the fire.

"Bernard?"

"Snooky?"

"Can I convince you to go to the sale tomorrow?"

"No."

"Are you sure?"

"Yes."

"Positive?"

"Yes."

Snooky sighed. "Nobody in this family is sociable except me," he said miserably.

The day of the rummage sale dawned bright and clear. It was a Saturday, and by ten-thirty in the morning there was a crowd gathered in front of the hall with the brightly colored sign RIDGEWOOD RUMMAGE SALE displayed across the door. Inside, Jessie was running back and forth like a demented hen. She yelled at her volunteers, "Lisa—Lisa—is your table all ready?—yes?—good—Henrietta—Henrietta, what's the matter over there?"

"Nothing, Miss Lowell," said Henrietta, who had spilled an entire bottle of nail polish on the English wool skirt and was desperately trying to clean it off before it hardened.

"All right. Are we ready, everyone?"

"Ready!"

"Albert? Gretchen? Everyone else? Man your stations!"

"We're ready, Jessie," said Gretchen impatiently. "Open the door."

Jessie unlocked the door and flung it open. She was nearly trampled by the hordes of humanity spilling into the hall. The crowd descended upon the tables en masse, throwing the carefully arranged clothing here and there, demanding prices, and bargaining in shrill tones. A startling transformation came over the bored, listless Henrietta. At the first sight of the crowd, her head came up and her nostrils flared widely. She took full charge of her table and began to bark out prices in a tone of authority. She made change quickly and expertly, counting the money out from a cigar box, and monitored any attempts to make off with unpurchased merchandise.

"Mrs. Hendrick," she yelled over the noise of the crowd, "Mrs. *Hendrick*, I don't believe you've paid me for that skirt, have you? Three dollars, please. That's right, three dollars. Oh, there's a tiny spot of nail polish on it, isn't there? All right, two dollars. Thank you very much. That blouse is going for ten dollars, Mrs. Ratliffe, it's pure silk. That's right. No, not a penny less. I'm sorry, Mrs. Ratliffe, but somebody else will buy it, then. Ten dollars is my final offer. That's right, my final offer. Thank you. Yes, I can make change."

The other teenage volunteer, Lisa, was giving way to tears.

"I am *not* overcharging you, Dr. Barton," she was saying. "That pair of hedge clippers is worth eight dollars. Yes, it is. Oh, Dr. Barton, how can you say that to me?"

Elsewhere in the room, there were cries of shocked dismay as various items, formerly given as presents, were found lying discounted on the tables.

"I gave you this cotton sweater last summer as a birthday present," one woman was saying furiously to another, a yellow sweater bunched in her hand. "How dare you, Eleanor? How dare you?"

The noise level in the room was almost unbearable as people screamed, bargained, and jostled each other in an attempt to get closer to the sale items. Snooky wiped his sweating face and wished he was anywhere but there. The room was crowded to capacity and he could barely hear the customers at his table as they screamed prices at him.

Jessie, at table number three, was managing to carry on an animated conversation with one of the mothers from her day-care center.

"So then I told him," she was saying as people ebbed and flowed around her, "I told him, 'Johnny, you have to share your fingerpaints with William now,' and do you know what he did, Mrs. Furness? He went right over like a little angel and shared them."

"That's my Johnny," said Johnny's mother. "He's a very giving person."

"Oh, my, yes. Why, as I told Gretchen the other day—fourteen dollars for that one, Mrs. Smith. No, I'm sorry, it's fourteen. Oh, all right, ten. That's fine. Did you pay for that, Ed? Ed?"

Ed, a disgruntled-looking silver-haired man, said he had.

"All right, I'm sorry. Don't be offended now. Don't go away mad. Anyway, as I was saying, Mrs. Furness . . ."

Mrs. Furness gave a whoop as she held up a blue

sequined evening gown. It glowed in rainbows of color in her hands. "Why, look at this!"

"Beautiful, isn't it? It's one of poor Mrs. Whitaker's dresses. Her daughter donated it. I really wasn't sure how much to ask—I'm sure it was terribly expensive when she bought it—"

A cunning look came into Johnny's mother's eyes. Bargaining began, and was successfully concluded a few minutes later. A sum of money changed hands, and both sides were satisfied.

"Thank you so much," said Jessie, closing the lid of the cigar box. "It's going to a good cause, you know that. Lovely dress, isn't it? Just your style, I would think. You know, looking at it reminds me . . . I was there the night she was killed, poor thing."

"What?" said Johnny's mother. The noise level had suddenly swelled around them.

"I WAS THERE," shouted Jessie. "THE NIGHT SHE WAS KILLED. POOR MRS. WHITAKER."

"OH, YES. TERRIBLE, WASN'T IT? MY HENRY SAID HE HAD NEVER HEARD OF SUCH A THING HAPPENING AROUND HERE."

"I KNOW," said Jessie. "UNBELIEVABLE, ISN'T IT? That's three dollars for that purse, thank you, Mrs. Kapleau," she said, suddenly diverted. "Thank you very much. Anyway, where was I? I was driving by the house that evening, and do you know, I saw the funniest thing . . . at least I *think* I saw it . . . maybe it was a trick of the light, or I could be wrong, I'm afraid my memory isn't what it used to be—"

"WHAT?"

Jessie repeated what she had said, but this time at the top of her lungs.

"AND THE STRANGE THING IS, IT JUST DOESN'T

MAKE ANY SENSE—I MEAN, I COULDN'T HAVE
SEEN WHAT I THOUGHT I SAW, BECAUSE THAT
WOULD MEAN THAT EVERYONE WAS THINKING
ABOUT IT COMPLETELY BACKWARDS—"

"Fascinating," said Mrs. Furness, who was no longer
listening. Her attention was riveted on a small sequined
purse. "How much is this handbag, Jessie? I could use
another evening bag. . . ."

By one o'clock, most of the items had been sold.
Snooky was slumped, exhausted, in his chair. So were
most of the other volunteers. Lisa was busily checking the
long list she had made of everything she had sold, and for
how much. A few items were missing without being paid
for.

"I don't know how people can do that," she said indignantly to no one in particular. "I don't understand it. It's
only a few dollars. Look at what's missing here: a hat, two
skirts, a letter opener, and that stupid white rabbit. I can't
believe anyone would want that rabbit enough to steal it.
It's not fair, honestly, it's just not fair."

Snooky was gazing with quiet pride at the items he had
managed to buy, in a few free moments allotted to him.
He had picked up a gray silk tie for Bernard, identical to
the other two that Bernard already owned, and a hat he
thought might fit him. For Maya he had scavenged a wool
skirt and an oversized white sweater. For himself he had
bought only the purple Ronald McDonald tie. He had
glimpsed it through the crowd and could not resist. Now
he knotted it wearily around his neck and said, "I wouldn't
worry, Lisa. Whoever took that wooden rabbit is cursed
enough."

"But it's not *fair*, Snooky. It's not right to steal."

"They can't mean to display it. Maybe somebody needed
firewood, have you thought of that?"

"Even so, they should have paid for it," said Lisa, who had a one-track mind. She went back to adding up columns of figures.

"Come on, George," said Susan wearily. "It's time to go."

"All right, Susan." George, in his free time, had managed to pick up four of his own shirts. Susan looked at him with fond despair.

"George, I don't believe you. You paid money for those shirts? George, there were some *nice* shirts on sale today. What about them?"

"I like these shirts, Susie. These are mine."

"Well, I bought these two for you. They're not great, but they're better than the ones you have. And this sweater is for Harold."

Albert was collapsed in his chair. He felt hot and tired. His good nature had been repeatedly abused by the shoppers, who had offered him less than he thought he should take but more than he felt he could refuse. He was positive he had taken in far less money than anybody else. Gretchen, at the table next to him, had been a model of efficiency. She was counting through her cigar box with a pleased expression on her face.

The room had emptied out a while ago, and now the volunteers began to stir, wearily lifting themselves from their chairs and hobbling toward the door.

"We'll come back later and clean the place up, Jessie," said Gretchen, closing the cigar box with a satisfied *click*. "All right?"

Jessie did not reply. She was sitting slumped in her chair, her head resting on her arm.

"Jessie?"

Snooky, almost at the door, looked back. In a few rapid strides he was next to Jessie. He bent over her.

The missing letter opener from Lisa's table was buried squarely in the center of Jessie's back.

Snooky straightened up·and his eyes met Albert's. Albert gave him a startled, questioning look. Gretchen began to scream, a high-pitched agonized sound.

"Jessie . . . oh, no . . . oh, God, no . . . !"

7

"Let me get this straight," said Bernard. "The woman was stabbed to death with one of the sale items sometime toward the end of the bazaar?"

"Yes." Snooky played listlessly with his Ronald McDonald tie.

"How do you know it was toward the end?"

"Because, Bernard, the three thousand women shouting prices at her half an hour earlier would probably have noticed if she was dead."

Bernard had to admit that was true. He leaned back and looked quietly out his study window. The willow tree in the backyard was bare, its branches whipping in the breeze.

"And she had seen something—the night your friend was killed?"

Snooky nodded. "That's what I gathered from what Gretchen was saying. She was nearly hysterical, and she kept on talking, talking, talking until the police came. She said Jessie had driven by the Whitaker house that night. It was dark out and she said at the time that she didn't see anything, but I guess she did. And there was something else—something about a Barbie doll Gretchen saw her playing with last night. She was walking it around on the floor and Gretchen said she seemed all funny about it."

"A Barbie doll," mused Bernard. "So Jessie saw someone going into the Whitaker house—someone who later said they weren't there . . . someone, perhaps, she wouldn't dream of suspecting, so she forgot all about it until last night—"

Their eyes met. Snooky nodded.

"Exactly," he said. "*Someone she wouldn't dream of suspecting . . .*"

The door opened and Maya came in. She had a worried, maternal expression on her face and was holding a steaming cup of brown liquid. "Here, Snooks. Drink this now." She thrust it at him.

Snooky eyed it dubiously. "What is it, My?"

"Just drink it and don't ask any questions. It's one of Bernard's new recipes."

Snooky gave a weak, trembly laugh. "Dog food, eh, Bernard?"

"Just do what your sister says and drink it, Snooky."

Snooky drank it. In between gulps he said,

"Hot cider, rum, a little brandy, orange juice, honey, cloves, cinnamon—hey, Bernard, this is the same as before, isn't it? Where was I? Honey, cloves, cinnamon . . ."

When he was done he said accusingly, "That wasn't any different."

"Yes, it was," said Bernard.

"Really?"

"Yes."

"There was something else in it?"

"Yes."

"Something I missed?"

"Yes."

"Not dog food again?"

"No."

"Oh. Then what was it?"

"Lethe," said Bernard.

"Lethe? What's lethe?"

"Forgetfulness, Snooky. Now go lie down and take a nap, will you?"

After Snooky had gone upstairs, Maya said, "There wasn't anything different in that recipe, was there, honey?"

"No. Just the power of suggestion."

"I see."

Maya sat down on the edge of Bernard's chair and he put his arm around her. "This is terrible, Bernard."

"Yes."

"It's so bad for Snooky to have to go through this. He has a sensitive nature, no matter what you say."

"It's worse for the people who were murdered."

"Yes. I know. I'm not forgetting them."

"I know."

They sat for a while in companionable silence. Twilight began to fill the room with a cold blue light. Maya leaned down to give her husband a kiss. "I'm going upstairs to check on him. Make sure he's asleep, and not tossing and turning. How are you doing? Should I turn on the lights as I go?"

"No."

She regarded him with the same anxious, maternal expression she usually saved for Snooky. "Are you all right?"

"I'm fine, Maya."

"What are you going to do now?"

"I'm going to think," said Bernard. "I'm going to think very, very hard."

After Maya had left, Bernard sat silently at his desk. The world outside turned blue in the early winter evening, then gray, then black. His form faded along with the light, until he was a silent motionless shape in the darkness. His mind was clicking along rapidly. A third murder . . . another person who had seen something or known something, and there could be a fourth or a fifth or a sixth before the killer finally felt safe.

He sat quietly for a long time, going over the whole affair from the beginning. Bernard had a precise, methodical mind, something that was not utilized a great deal in his profession, which called more on his reserves of intuition and creativity. Now he went over everything that had happened in detail. Bella's death . . . Mrs. MacGregor's death . . . *something she didn't see* . . . the earring . . .

who planted it on him? . . . Jessie Lowell's death . . . *who was it she had seen?* . . .

Bernard stirred and sighed. Under the desk, Misty raised her head and gave him a reproachful look which he could not see in the darkness. He felt annoyed with himself. There was something that Snooky had said recently; something that had stuck in Bernard's mind, if only he could recall it; something that had gone by unnoticed at the time, but now was prickling at him like a thorn, announcing itself and its own importance . . .

He remembered Aunt Etta sitting like a mushroom on the hard sofa in her living room, saying, "She shut her mouth and wouldn't say anything except that it didn't make any sense. . . ."

It didn't make any sense.

Of course nothing about this case did make much sense.

If only he could remember what Snooky had said. It was an offhand comment, one of Snooky's specialties, and Snooky himself, as usual, had no idea what he was actually saying. . . .

For a long time there was complete silence in the study, except for the sound of Misty's gentle snores. Suddenly Bernard gave a loud grunt. Misty moved and grumbled at his feet.

Bernard grunted again; he sounded happy. He turned on the lamp, took out his notebook and carefully printed:

F SH HD GN T THT NT

Then he put down the Magic Marker and began to think even harder than before.

* * *

Detective Janovy was feeling very frazzled. Jessie Lowell was dead. He thought he knew why someone had killed her, but he still did not know who that killer was. Half the citizens of Ridgewood were on his back, protesting that *they* could have been killed, and that an insane murderer was on the loose in their quiet town. One thing Janovy was sure of, in this case where he was not sure of anything, was that the killer was not insane. Jessie Lowell had been killed because she knew something, and she had chosen to announce that fact at the top of her voice in a crowded room.

Still, having a murder take place during the rummage sale was bad for the sale (most of the citizenry had sworn off ever going there again), bad for Ridgewood, and bad for everyone involved. Whoever was doing this was quick-witted, thought Janovy for the hundredth time. He or she had seen their chance and taken it, while the room was still crowded and everyone's attention was focused on the sale items. The murderer had chosen an opportune moment, when the room was full enough, but not so full that Jessie's apparent fatigue would be noticed and remarked upon.

Mrs. Furness, little Johnny's mother, was having heart palpitations. She sat in Janovy's closetlike office and gestured with wide sweeping motions of her hands, nearly knocking Fish out the door.

"I was standing right there next to her," she was saying. "*Right there,* I'm telling you. How awful! The murderer could have been anywhere . . . right behind us . . . I'm telling you, it gives me the trembles to think of it. A murderer standing behind me. My heart isn't very strong, you know."

Detective Janovy was of the private opinion that Mrs.

Furness's heart was as strong as a mule's, but he did not contradict her.

"Not strong at all," Mrs. Furness went on with evident pride. "Why, just the other day the doctor was telling me that I should avoid any shocks to my system—I'm telling you, this could have *killed* me."

"Yes. Yes. Terrible. Tell me, Mrs. Furness, what exactly did Jessie Lowell say to you?"

Mrs. Furness hemmed and hawed, obviously preferring to discuss the state of her cardiovascular system, but finally got down to brass tacks.

". . . and then she said it didn't make any sense and she thought everyone was thinking about it completely backwards," she finished in triumph. "At least, I *think* that was what she said. I wasn't giving her my total attention, you see—it was so loud there, and as a matter of fact there was this darling little evening bag I had my eye on—"

Janovy and Fish exchanged glances. "Thank you very much for coming by with this information," Janovy said. "We appreciate it, Mrs. Furness."

She fairly bristled with self-satisfaction.

"Of course, Officer. I felt it was my civic duty."

She shook hands with both of them and left.

Janovy leaned back in his chair and said, " 'Everyone was thinking about it completely backwards.' Any idea what she meant by that, Fish?"

"No, sir."

"Could she mean there's another suspect—one we haven't thought of?"

"I don't know, sir."

Janovy did not know either. It made him very uneasy.

"Any fingerprints on that letter opener, Fish?"

"No, sir. It had been wiped clean."

Janovy nodded wearily. "What are we down to, Fish? We can't wait until they're all killed off before we have a suspect." He ticked off the names on his fingers. "Albert and Susan Whitaker, Gretchen Schneider, George Drexler. Etta Pinsky wasn't at the sale yesterday, and anyway she has no apparent motive for any of these murders. George Drexler couldn't have killed Bella Whitaker, but he might be in on it with Susan. Albert and Gretchen might be working together, as well. What do you think, Fish? Are we looking for one person working alone, or for a team?"

Fish looked more mournful than ever and said he didn't know. It was a strange case. It didn't quite meet the eye.

Janovy agreed wholeheartedly. It didn't meet the eye. The more he found out, the more complicated it seemed.

The whole business worried him.

He rose to his feet and said, "I want to talk to Gretchen Schneider."

He looked with compassion at the tall sticklike figure in front of him. In the course of a few hours, Gretchen seemed to have aged several years. Her face was ravaged, swollen red with tears. Albert, sitting by her side in the Whitaker living room, looked absolutely deflated, collapsed in upon himself. His fair hair stuck out wildly in all directions, and his big square face looked drained and empty. He had taken off his glasses, and his eyes looked strangely unfocused.

"I'll do anything," Gretchen was saying in a low tone, "anything it takes to catch the person who killed her. Do you hear me, Detective—*anything*."

"Yes, thank you, Dr. Schneider." In his mind's eye, Janovy had a sudden uneasy vision of citizen vigilantes riding wildly through the night. He did not like the haunted look on Gretchen's pale face and the weird fire that burned in her eyes. "Thank you. You understand we're doing our best to find out who it was. Now, can you tell me anything— anything at all that you think might have a bearing on why Miss Lowell was killed?"

Gretchen told him, in a few terse words, about the conversation she had had with Jessie the night before the bazaar.

"She was looking at this doll, and she seemed very odd. I stopped and asked her how she was, and she looked right through me. She seemed to be thinking hard about something."

That was all that Gretchen knew. No, Jessie had been fine later that evening, when they came home together. And she had been her usual bossy self, the day of the bazaar. Tears sprang to Gretchen's eyes.

"I didn't see her during the bazaar at all. She was at table number three, and I was at table number six."

"Can you tell me who had the tables on either side of her?"

"Oh, yes, let me think. George was on one side of her, at table number two, and that tall young man with the funny name, what is it now, Snooky Randolph, was on the other side. Susan was beyond George at table one, and now let me see, who was at table five . . . ?"

"I was," said Albert.

"Oh, yes, that's right, dear. You were. And on the other side of me were the two teenagers, Henrietta and Lisa, at tables seven and eight. But I'm afraid that's not very helpful, Detective Janovy. The tables were arranged in a circle, after all, so table eight was right next to table one. And the noise level was incredible. You had to be there to believe it. Even someone at the next table couldn't

have heard Jessie talking. It would have had to be someone who was right near her."

"Even if she was shouting?"

"Yes. Even if she was shouting. Isn't that so, Albert?"

Albert woke up from a kind of stupor he had fallen
into. "Oh. Yes. Yes, you couldn't hear anything. The room
was filled with screaming women."

"All the volunteers got some free time away from their
tables?"

"Yes," said Gretchen. "Ten minutes. It was staggered
so that two people wouldn't be off at the same time."

"I see."

Albert's story was the same as Gretchen's. He had
been busy during the sale—overwhelmed, he said—and
hadn't seen Jessie at all.

"Thank you, Dr. Whitaker."

Albert escorted the detectives to the front door and
took their coats out of the closet. "Gretchen will be staying
here with me, Detective Janovy. I'm not having her go
back to that house alone. She's going to live here with me
until we're married."

"I understand."

So the two of them were getting married, thought
Janovy as he and Fish went down the icy steps toward
their car. That was interesting. It didn't seem right, did it?
Marriage in the midst of all this death.

No, it didn't seem quite right.

He got in and sat in the passenger seat as Fish started
the car. Janovy sat for a long time, not moving, sunk in
thought. So Jessie Lowell had seen who had gone into the
Whitaker house that night. It was perhaps just a glimpse,
but it was sufficient. The porch light was on and she had
seen someone. And, perhaps more importantly, the per-

son she had seen was almost definitely a woman. She had been looking at a female doll and it had jogged her memory.

A woman, thought Janovy. Well, there were only three women involved in this case: Aunt Etta, Susan, and Gretchen herself. Aunt Etta he discounted. She had neither motive nor opportunity for these crimes. Both Susan's and Gretchen's motives, on the other hand, were obvious.

So he had it down to two, Janovy thought. Two people. But that wasn't good enough. He still didn't *know*. . . .

Bernard was looking doubtfully at a page of his notes. In green ink, he had written several lines that he was sure were important if he could only remember what it was he had meant. The lines read:

RNG MT B MPRTNT—MT N MN WT SMS T MN H BT KY?
And at the bottom:
GNGS BRM

"Gngs brm," Bernard said experimentally, rolling the sounds over and over his tongue. "Gnnngs brmmmm. Gnngggsss . . . goings? Goings brm? Goings brimmm. Broommm. Brummm. No. Hmmmm . . ."

This was the problem with his system of shorthand, one which he had never yet solved. Usually saying the words out loud made a difference, but today he could not figure out what he had meant at all.

But it didn't really matter. He knew, anyway. He knew who was behind all the murders.

Bernard sat back and looked thoughtfully out his window. There was nothing to be seen except smooth, empty blackness. He felt upset. There was only one way all the facts made sense . . . but that was not proof. Unless someone did something, the killer would get away with it. And *that* Bernard did not approve of at all. No. He did not like the thought of somebody literally getting away with murder.

With three murders . . . and sixty-four million dollars . . .

He shook himself all over, like a dog, then got up and went upstairs to the third floor. Misty trailed behind, hoping against hope that it was time for dinner. Bernard knocked on the door of the guest bedroom and Snooky's voice called out, "Come in, whoever you may be."

Snooky was sitting swathed in blankets and propped up by pillows on the bed. He had his chin in his hand and was staring out the window, something he spent a lot of time doing. ("I can't explain it, Maya," he had told her once when she asked him what in the world he was thinking about. "I need time every day just to stare. I can't explain it.") Now he said, "Bernard, what a pleasure. Please come or in. Pull up a chair. Notice how cold it is, and notice also that I have not complained in a long time. What brings you here? Just wanted a trip up to the arctic circle?"

Bernard pulled up a rickety wooden chair and sat down.

"Can I offer you a blanket against the cold?"

"No, thank you."

"You never feel the cold, do you, Bernard?"

"No."

Snooky looked at him enviously. "It must be the physique. You're like a bear, did you know that? I wouldn't be surprised if you hibernated."

"Snooky."

"Yes?"

"Please try to concentrate. I need you to call that pet detective of yours, what's his name, Anchovy—"

"Janovy."

"—and suggest a few things to him. Would you be willing to do that?"

"Well, why not? But why would he listen to me? What do I know about anything?"

"He'll listen," said Bernard, "when you tell him who killed Bella Whitaker."

Detective Janovy, with his faithful shadow Fish, knocked on the door of the ancient white-and-blue Victorian. Snooky let them in, and ushered them upstairs to Bernard's study.

The two detectives were closeted with Bernard for nearly an hour. Downstairs, Snooky fidgeted and fretted.

"I don't see why I'm being left out of it," he said to his sister, who was sitting placidly proofreading one of her own articles. "I mean, Bella was *my* friend, wasn't she? If it weren't for me, Bernard wouldn't even be involved in this. What does he know about it, anyway? He barely knows these people."

"Bernard is very prescient," said Maya, calmly correcting a spelling error.

"Prescient? Prescient? You mean he has ESP?"

"No, Snooky. I mean he's very good at analyzing things and predicting how they'll come out. He doesn't need to know people well in order to analyze patterns. He's very good at getting the bigger view of things. Take Aunt Martha, for example. You remember Aunt Martha?"

Snooky strained his eyes upward. "Aunt Martha? Elderly blue-haired lady? Strongly resembles a toad?"

"That's her. Well, you remember when we had a big

housewarming party when we moved in? You were here. You drank an entire bowl of champagne punch."

"I remember. Pink bubbly stuff, with fruit floating in it. It was delicious."

"Anyway, the next day we found out that some of our best crystal was missing. Wedding presents, some things I inherited, all kinds of stuff. Bernard said that Aunt Martha had taken them. I asked her for them, and she was very nice about it. She said she couldn't imagine how it had happened, and she gave everything back. To this day I don't know how Bernard guessed. The only time he ever met her was at that party, and there were at least fifteen other people here."

"So you're telling me that my Aunt Martha is a kleptomaniac?"

"That's right. We talked about it for a long time. She's very sweet. She said she would have given everything back the next day, except that there was one crystal nightingale on a branch that she had set her heart on, and she couldn't bear to part with it."

"Touching story. I hope you turned her over to the police?"

"I gave her the nightingale."

Snooky looked disgusted. "Sucker," he said.

"She's a relative, Snooky. Not unlike yourself."

"I don't steal from you."

"Just room and board," said Maya, but with vast affection. She leaned forward and patted his hand. "Don't worry about Aunt Martha. We had her over a few times after that, and she never took a thing. Not a single thing."

"That's hardly an achievement, Maya. Most guests don't steal things when you invite them over."

"It's an achievement for Aunt Martha," said Maya tartly.

"So how did Bernard know?"

Maya shrugged. A puzzled look came over her face. "I tried to get him to talk about it, but all he said was that it was the look in her eyes. I don't know what that means. He's not terribly verbal, you know."

"You're kidding. Bernard? Not verbal?"

"Perhaps you've noticed this."

"I've noticed that he never talks to me if he can help it."

"You always take everything so personally, Snooks. You know Bernard never talks to anyone if he can help it. It's part of his charm."

"A large part," said Snooky gloomily.

Upstairs, in the study, Detective Janovy was shaking his head.

"I don't know," he said slowly. "I don't know. It seems fantastic."

"It's the only way all the facts fit," said Bernard.

Janovy nodded. "It would take a great deal of planning."

"Certainly. This was a well-planned crime. Nothing rash or impulsive about it, except for Jessie Lowell's murder. There the murderer saw that she knew something, had seen something, and had to be gotten out of the way quickly."

Janovy nodded thoughtfully. It *did* fit. And it reverberated with his deepest instincts, which had told him all along that these crimes were the result of long and careful planning.

"The point is, what are you going to do about it?" said Bernard.

Janovy sat back and stared out the window. "This plan of yours. It's tricky. We could be setting ourselves up.

How positive are you that the person we want isn't Gretchen Schneider?"

"I'm not sure," replied Bernard, "but I think the probabilities are against it. I don't believe that she would have killed Jessie Lowell under any circumstances. It would be too easy for her to convince Jessie that she was wrong in what she saw. She has a motive for all these crimes, of course, but I don't believe it's her."

Janovy nodded again.

"One more thing," said Bernard. He got up, opened the study door, and went to the head of the stairs. "Snooky?"

His brother-in-law came bounding upstairs like a gazelle. "Yes? Yes, Bernard? What is it?"

"Come inside."

Snooky was ushered inside and the door closed again. The sound of voices could be heard rising and falling from within. Downstairs, Maya red-penciled another mistake in her article and smiled to herself. Ever since he was little, Snooky could not bear being left out of anything. If there was a tree-house club anywhere in the neighborhood that he did not belong to, it would drive him crazy. When he was older, it was parties—he had an uncanny gift for knowing where and when a party was going on, and he had been known to crash diplomatic functions and vice-presidential receptions, once he had honed this ability into a fine art. But to Maya it would always be the tree-house mentality. She remembered how he had cried one summer—cried in complete and utter desolation—when some of the neighborhood boys had organized an insect-collecting club and he had not been allowed to join. The fact that he actually loathed insects had not made any difference. When the boys finally got around to asking him, he had accepted happily and spent the rest of the summer refusing to go on any of their collecting trips.

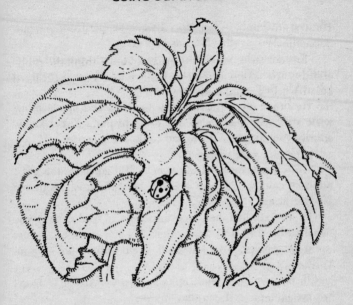

Anything bigger than a spider gave him the willies, he told Maya. He was eventually kicked out of the club, but that did not bother him at all. The important thing was that he had once, however briefly, belonged.

Maya smiled to herself and turned the page.

The next day, a car pulled up in front of the Whitaker mansion, and Bernard and Detective Janovy got out. Gretchen met them at the door and led the way into the living room. There she sat down and listened carefully to what Bernard told her. He spoke shortly and succinctly, wasting no words. She was intelligent, as he had known, and long before he was done her mouth had compressed itself into a thin severe line.

When he was finished, she sat silently, her hands

playing restlessly in her lap. "I understand. I understand. Yes, Mr. Woodruff. I'll do as you say."

"You see why we're coming to you," interposed Detective Janovy. "Your friendship with Jessie Lowell makes it plausible that—"

He broke off. Gretchen was nodding, and her face had gone very white. She said in a low whisper, "Yes. I know. I'll do it for Jessie. I'll be glad to do it for Jessie."

"When?" asked Bernard.

Gretchen glanced at her watch. "I'll go there tonight," she said calmly. "No use beating about the bush, is there? No use at all."

Janovy studied her face anxiously. "You're sure you can handle this, Dr. Schneider? It's not without an element of danger, you know. If you'd rather not get involved . . ."

"I *am* involved," she replied sharply. "Aren't I? Don't worry, Detective. I can play my part."

Bernard got to his feet. "Just don't strangle anyone or attack anyone," he said mildly. "There have been enough murders as it is."

Gretchen looked at him, and a spark of gallows humor lit up her face. "Yes," she said. "There have been enough murders."

Albert, who had been excluded from their meeting, was fretting the same way Snooky had been fretting. After the two men had left, he went into the living room and said, "Gretchen? Are you all right? What did they want?"

"I'm fine, Albert. I'm fine." She was sitting gazing thoughtfully out into the garden, which was covered with frost. The oval flower bed looked like a grave today, she thought.

"What did they want?"

"They asked me to do something, Albert. Something for Jessie. I'm going to do it, and I don't want you to stop me."

"Is it dangerous?"

"Not if I play it right." Her hands twisted and untwisted nervously on her lap. "Not if I play it right."

He sat down next to her and took her hands into his own, stilling their movement. "How can I help?" he asked humbly.

"Oh, Albert." Her lined, worried, haunted face grew softer as she gazed at him. "You're too good for me, Albert. You really are."

He was frowning to himself. "I don't like this," he said sharply. "Why can't you tell me what's going on? What is this?"

"Don't badger me, Albert. I need to think." She took her hands away from his, and turned away to gaze out at the frost-covered garden again. Strange how that flower bed resembled a grave . . . she would have to do something about that in the spring. . . .

"I need to *think*," she said curtly.

8

That evening, when Susan came home from a movie that she and George had taken Harold to see—*Nine Thousand Ways to Die*, a cult science fiction classic that Harold had already seen practically nine thousand times—she found Snooky shivering on her doorstep.

"Snooky, what are you doing here? I told you we wouldn't be home until eight-thirty, didn't I? Have you been waiting long?"

"No, no."

"Come inside and get warm. You look half frozen. Harold, where are your mittens? Harold, look at me, young man. What have you done with your mittens?"

"I ate them," Harold said sullenly.

"All right, go inside, young man. They must be around somewhere. George, would you look in the car? Do you see Harold's mittens?"

George was locking up the car. "No, I don't," he said absently. "Listen, Susie, you know the part where the aliens communicate through those toothbrush things they had on the top of their heads? You remember that? What were those things, anyway?"

"They were toothbrushes, George. This was the lowest-budget science ficton film I've ever seen," she told Snooky. "The alien space ship looked exactly like a bottle cap. Didn't it, George? It looked like a soda bottle cap, shot from up close."

"But those toothbrush things—"

"That reminds me. HAROLD, BRUSH YOUR TEETH BEFORE YOU GET INTO BED. I'M SERIOUS, YOUNG MAN. I CAN TELL THE DIFFERENCE, YOU KNOW. THOSE CHOCOLATE GOOBERS ARE BAD FOR YOUR TEETH. Do you think he heard me, George?"

"I think they heard you in Wisconsin, Susie. Now listen, do you remember the part where the aliens pointed those things at people and they fell down? What were those things?"

"I don't know. They looked like garden rakes to me. Deadly garden rakes. You know, the long kind with the hooked part on the end. The alien leader looked like he was wearing a roll of toilet paper on his head. It worries me that Harold likes this film so much, Georgie. What does it mean?"

"It's okay, Susan. I think it gets his aggression out. He always seems calmer after we see it."

"Really? Do you think so?"

"Excuse me," said Snooky. "Susan, can I talk to you for a minute?"

Susan looked contrite. "I'm sorry, Snooky. What is it? Would you like something hot to drink?"

"No. It's something . . . well, sort of personal. A relationship problem. You know how I always turned to your mother for advice, and now that she's gone—well, I wondered if I could talk to you about it."

"Oh. Of course. I'll just put Harold to bed, and then you and I can talk in the kitchen. You don't mind, do you, George?"

"No, Susie, no, no, no, you go right ahead. I've got some stuff I have to do here anyway."

Susan put Harold to bed, surprisingly without too many protests on his part ("Maybe George is right," she thought, "he does seem, well, *calmer* than usual"). It worried her that Harold liked that low-budget alien movie so much— why couldn't he enjoy *Pinocchio* and *101 Dalmatians* like other children his age?—but there was no denying that he seemed happy and content. He took his old, worn, much-loved teddy bear into bed with him and fell asleep practically immediately, his blond head tucked underneath the pillow, the way he always slept. She had given up years ago worrying that he would somehow smother himself.

When she came back into the kitchen, Snooky was sitting idly thumbing through a tabloid magazine. "Look at this," he said. "PREACHER EXPLODES IN PULPIT AFTER FIRE-AND-BRIMSTONE SERMON. What is this, Susan? Do you read this stuff?"

"I can't help it. Dora brings it over and leaves it here. She buys three different kinds every week. I know it's terrible, but I've started reading them. Look at this—EIGHTY-SIX-YEAR-OLD WOMAN GIVES BIRTH TO TWINS. What do you think? Where do they get this stuff?"

"I don't know. I can't imagine. My horoscope says I shouldn't have gotten out of bed today. Yours says you shouldn't make any new business deals."

Susan handed him a cup of steaming hot chocolate. "Now, what's this terrible problem of yours?"

"Oh. Right. Well, it's like this. My girlfriend left me a while ago for one of her professors, which is depressing enough, but she recently wrote to tell me she's getting married, to this guy who's at least twice her age. Consciously I wish them all the best, but I keep on having this disturbing dream where I firebomb their wedding and everybody goes up in flames, except for Deirdre, who lives long enough to beg my forgiveness and tell me I'm the only man she's ever really loved."

"And then she dies?"

"Oh, yes, they all die, especially the professor, who goes up like a torch. And then there's this other dream I've been having where Deirdre turns into this enormous frog and keeps trying to tell me something, but I can't understand what she's saying because it's just this weird kind of hoarse croak, you know. . . ."

Outside Susan's little blue-and-yellow house, a car pulled up and Gretchen got out. She walked up the front steps and rang the doorbell. Nothing happened, so she rang again. After a minute or two, George opened the door. He looked flustered, and a viola string hung from his hand.

"I'm sorry," he said. "I was listening to the opera, and of course you can't hear anything at all through that. Come on in."

"Thank you."

He led her into the tiny, cluttered living room, where he picked up his viola and began to thread the string into the peg. "Restringing the instrument," he said by way of explanation. "Have to do it every so often. Good for the morale, too, the viola sounds so much better. Is the opera too loud?"

Gretchen thought the banshee sounds emanating from the speakers were far too loud, but she sat down with her hands folded and said politely, "Oh, no, of course not."

George grinned at her. "Yes, it is," he said, and lowered the volume. "You're here to see Susan? I'm afraid she's busy right now. She's talking with Snooky in the kitchen."

"That's all right," said Gretchen. "I can wait."

"Oh, good."

Gretchen sat there quietly for a few minutes, watching George as he bent over his task. He looked so gentle, so essentially harmless, sitting there, she thought. His long stringy dark hair fell over his forehead, his thin fingers wrestled with the string, and his eyes were half-closed with concentration. A soprano aria came booming out of the speakers, and George sang along in a high tinny voice totally unlike his own. His whole being was focused on the viola string. She watched him for a little while, then grasped her hands together and said abruptly,

"George, *I know you did it.*"

"Did what?" He looked up and smiled at her in a sleepy, startlingly sensual way. She began to see what Susan had seen in him, something that had always eluded her before. The string had held, and now he picked up the next one and began to thread it carefully through the peg.

"George, please. I know that you killed all those people. I know it was you."

He looked up again. She thought he looked faintly wary. "Gretchen, if this is your idea of a joke, then it isn't in very good taste."

"It's not a joke. Believe me, it's not a joke. There's nothing funny about it."

"No, there isn't." He put aside the viola and sat up, hugging his knees. There was a strained silence between them. The voice of a basso profundo boomed out of the speakers. George reached out with a lazy gesture and switched off the tape.

"What is it, Gretchen?" he said. "What's the matter? What have you really come to talk about?"

"I've come to talk to you about Jessie," she said quietly.

"Jessie?"

"Jessie had guessed it was you, the night before you killed her, George. She found a Barbie doll in a box some people had donated, and it jogged her memory. You didn't know that she drove by Bella Whitaker's house that night, did you? Nobody did, except for me and the police. Jessie said all along that she hadn't seen anything, that the porch light was on but the rest of the place was dark and she couldn't see anything. She just drove by for a moment and didn't think about it much afterwards. But as it turned out, she had seen something—hadn't she, George? She saw the one thing you were afraid people would find out, and that's why you killed her, isn't it?" She paused, her hands working nervously in her lap. "The doll reminded her. *She had seen Bella Whitaker leaving the house that night.* Oh, maybe just a quick glimpse of her walking down the steps as Jessie drove by, just a flash out of the side of her eyes, but she saw it, all right. She saw Bella Whitaker leaving—or rather, being *forced* to leave, isn't that right, George? She saw her being forced down the front steps with stiff, jerky movements, *just like that doll.*"

Gretchen leaned forward. Her face was very white now. George stared at her as if fascinated. His mouth hung slightly open and his eyes were wide.

"Nobody guessed it was you, George, because of your alibi. At the time that Bella died, you were miles away, in Springfield, at a concert. But the truth is, *so was Bella.* Everyone assumed that because she was found at home, she was murdered at home. But that's not the way it was, was it? You drove her to that concert, and you killed her there and hid her body in your car."

George stared at her, his eyes faintly bulging. He said nothing.

Gretchen gave a faint, half-hysterical laugh. "That's why that stupid earring was under your car seat, wasn't it, George? Nobody hid it there. Nobody planted it on you. It fell off of Bella's ear when she was struggling with you, while you were strangling her. It fell off and rolled under the seat.

"You were so clever all along, George. Really, if Jessie hadn't told me enough of what she had seen, the night before she died, I would never have been able to piece it together. Old Mrs. MacGregor . . . she didn't know who had done it, but she knew one thing that you couldn't afford to have her tell anyone. It was the coat, wasn't it, George? The mink coat? Mrs. MacGregor had gone out to the front hall closet at six-thirty that evening, and she had opened the closet for her coat, and she had seen something. Or rather, she had *not* seen something. *She had seen that Bella's black mink coat wasn't there.* Which was peculiar, really, because Bella was supposed to have never left the house. Yet where could the coat be? It was a freezing cold night—Bella would never have left without it. Mrs. MacGregor didn't know what it meant, but she knew it was important. She had a knack for that kind of thing. But she was stupid. She didn't realize how important it really was. And so you killed her."

Gretchen leaned back. She felt suddenly drained and exhausted.

"Of course the coat wasn't there," she said, "because Bella had already left with you in your car. The sound of the door opening and closing that Mrs. MacGregor heard wasn't the sound of someone coming in—it was the sound of both of you *leaving*, wasn't it? By the time Mrs. MacGregor came out to get her coat, the house was empty. When did you actually come into the house, George— earlier in the afternoon?"

There was a silence. From the kitchen they could hear the faint sound of Snooky's voice droning on.

"Yes," said George. His eyes were half-closed now, and his thin face wore a sleepy, pleased look. "Around five-thirty."

"And you waited . . . under the stairs?"

"Yes." George picked up his viola again and absent-mindedly played with the string. "It didn't take very long. She came downstairs about forty-five minutes later."

"And then you came up behind her . . . ?"

"And I slipped a rope around her neck and pulled it tight enough so she couldn't talk. Then I told her to stay quiet and come with me," said George in his soft voice. His eyes were closed now as he relived the memory. "I took her out to the car and I talked to her all the way to Springfield. I gave her one last chance. I told her she was being unreasonable. I told her Susan and I loved each other, and I begged her not to cut us out of the will."

"What did she say?"

George shrugged indifferently. "She laughed at me. She wasn't frightened at all. She just laughed."

"And then . . ." Gretchen's voice trailed away.

"And then I parked the car in an indoor garage underneath the concert hall, and when she went to get out, I killed her."

"With the rope?" asked Gretchen in a whisper.

"Yes. She never knew what was happening. I knew Susan wouldn't want her to suffer."

Gretchen felt perversely fascinated. It was just as Bernard had said. . . . "And then you hid her body in the car—"

"—and went upstairs and played the concert," said George Drexler. He opened his eyes and smiled at her. "No one knew! That's what got me, the entire time. Nobody even knew! And then, when the concert was over, I got in the car and drove her home. It was awkward, getting her out of the car and everything, but she wasn't stiff yet. It had only been a few hours. I was safe enough, I knew Albert wouldn't be home until after midnight. Right, Gretchen? You're like clockwork, the two of you. Going out every Friday night for years and years."

"How did you get into the house, George? Where did you get the key?" Gretchen asked in a whisper. She was frightened now. She could feel her whole body trembling. The hairs on the back of her neck were standing up. Here, she felt, was the authentic presence of evil: this sleepy-faced man who was so eagerly telling her how he had murdered his fiancée's mother. . . .

George smiled at her. It was his usual sweet, pleasant smile. "I had copies made of Susie's keys, of course. It was easy. The whole thing was so easy. I arranged her on the floor with the rope next to her. The whole point was that nobody would ever know that she had been out of the house. I didn't notice that one of her earrings was missing, though," he said thoughtfully. He chewed his lip. "That was stupid of me. I was in quite a state, though. I had never murdered anyone before."

"Really, George?"

"Really."

There was a long silence. They stared at each other. From behind the closed kitchen door, they could hear Snooky saying, "And then this *other* recurrent dream I've been having . . ."

Finally George said earnestly, "I never wanted to kill anyone, Gretchen. Honestly. You have to believe me. It's just that I didn't feel I had any choice. Bella was being impossible about our marriage, and I didn't want to deprive Susan of all that money."

"Susan? Or yourself?"

He shrugged. "Me, too, I guess. I'm tired of being poor. I've always been poor, just scraping by, trying to make a living and play my viola as much as I can. If I were rich, I could play all the time . . . I could even form my own group."

"Philo George?" Gretchen said, and stifled a half-hysterical impulse to giggle.

"More or less." He smiled at her. "I'm not that egotistical, Gretchen. But I could play when I wanted and where I wanted. It would be on my own terms, and I wouldn't have to worry about the money anymore. I thought I could have one clean murder, no strings attached. But it wasn't like that. It didn't turn out that way at all." He looked past her, chewing his lip. "It got so *messy*," said George Drexler, rather pathetically, like a child. "All these people seeing something, or me being afraid all the time that somebody *had* seen something . . . damn Mrs. MacGregor! Who would have guessed that she'd remember about the coat? And then when that earring rolled out from under the car seat, and Susan was right there, I nearly died. Honestly, I nearly died. Thank God all of you had been in the car right before that. I don't know *how* I would have explained it otherwise."

Gretchen suddenly felt that she was addressing a wayward student. There was something about the way George was sitting there, talking to her so reasonably . . . her fear fell away. She gathered up her handbag and said severely, "You've been a very bad boy, George. You know that."

"Yes, Gretchen. I know."

"You've killed three people."

"I know. I know." George bent his head.

"I came here tonight to see if Jessie was right," said Gretchen thoughtfully. "She hinted to me that it might have been you . . . once she realized that Bella hadn't been at home that evening, then your own alibi got you into trouble, George. Everybody else was here in Ridgewood that evening, except for you. Except for *you.*"

"I know."

Gretchen's mouth thinned into a stern uncompromising line. "I don't have any proof, of course. Nothing that would stand up in court. Nothing that would convince the police. But there's one thing I'm going to do, for Albert's sake, and that is to make sure that Susan knows the whole story. Jessie would have wanted that. It's not right that you should marry into the family. You understand that, don't you?"

George's head came up. "Yes," he said woodenly.

"Good-bye, George," said Gretchen. She got to her feet.

George stood up also. "Good-bye," he said.

As she turned to go, George's hand rose swiftly, and a thin metal string arched through the air. It fell around Gretchen's throat, and then George was next to her, holding it and twisting, twisting it tighter and tighter . . .

Gretchen tried to scream and couldn't. She clawed at her neck, at the metal thread that was biting into her skin . . . everything was going blue . . . she reached out blindly, groping through the air, and scratched George's face as viciously as she could.

George reeled back with a scream. The front door flew open, and a firm hand clamped down on his arm. All of a sudden the room seemed filled with people. He felt the barrel of a revolver being placed firmly against his temple.

"Now, now, Mr. Drexler," said Detective Janovy's voice pleasantly. "Don't move, please, or I might be tempted to put a bullet through your head in the line of duty. Are you sure you're all right, Dr. Schneider?"

9

"What tipped you off, Bernard? How did you know that Bella wasn't murdered at home? What gave you the clue?"

"You did, Snooky."

"Me? I did?"

"Yes."

Snooky felt absurdly pleased. "What did I say?"

"You mumbled something, in one of your ceaseless monologues, about how, if she had gone out that night, she would have been the most stylish woman in the restaurant. Don't you remember?"

"Yes. No. I guess so."

"The phrase came back to me later," said Bernard slowly. "*If she had gone out that night*. It would make sense out of a lot of things. Like the earring, which made no sense at all otherwise. Why would the killer take it? But if Bella had been out that night, then it might have fallen off her ear—*in George's car*—and shown up later, by accident. That, and his alibi, pointed straight at George."

Snooky was thoughtful. "I see. Clever of you, Bernard.

How did you figure out what in the world Mrs. MacGregor was hinting about?"

"Occam's razor," said Bernard shortly.

"I see," said Snooky. "Simplicity is all, eh, Bernard?"

"Yes. When choosing among competing theories, choose the simplest one. It was obvious that something about the black mink coat had triggered Mrs. MacGregor's memory. She said so herself, to Aunt Etta. The simplest explanation would be that it was the *coat itself* that had been missing. And that tied in so neatly with Bella Whitaker leaving the house that night, that I knew that must be it."

Snooky looked at him in frank admiration. "That's so—so *cogent* of you, Bernard."

Bernard merely scowled.

Maya, from across the table, passed her brother a slice of pie. "So in a way, Snookers, you could say that you helped Bernard figure it out."

"I don't know, Maya. It's not like what I did was *conscious* or anything."

"Anyone who talks as much as Snooky does is bound to say something intelligent sooner or later," said Bernard. "Please pass the pie, Maya."

There was a happy silence as they ate the blueberry pie.

"Bernard's beating us, Maya," said Snooky, eyeing his brother-in-law's plate. "He always does beat us. I can never understand how he eats so fast."

"I have a compound stomach," remarked Bernard sourly, "not unlike a cow."

"How is Gretchen?" asked Maya.

"She's okay," replied Snooky. "Albert was there and he took care of her. She was all shaken up, of course, but she's going to be fine."

"And Susan?"

"Well, when she heard all the commotion she opened the door and went dashing out of the kitchen. Just in time, too. I was running out of dreams. The last one I came up with, Deirdre was a gigantic whale and I was a big purple balloon floating among the stars."

"Did she diagnose you as psychotic?"

"No, but I think she was beginning to look very worried."

"How's she handling everything?" asked Maya.

"Not too well, actually. She says she'll never get married again."

Maya nodded. "Well, she thinks that right now. She won't always feel that way."

Snooky regarded his sister curiously. "Really? That's interesting. When did you become a seer?"

"I just happen to know about marriage, that's all. Nearly everyone settles down sooner or later. Not everyone is like you, you know, Snooks. Most people *want* a relationship."

Snooky was offended. "I want a relationship."

"You only want bad ones."

"I don't want bad ones, Maya, they're just the only ones that seem to happen to me."

His sister shrugged. "You could have a decent relationship with a woman if you really wanted to."

"You think so? Really?"

"Absolutely. You're afraid of settling down. It's very simple, Snooks. You have a deep-seated fear of attachment."

"I enjoy being psychoanalyzed over dessert," Snooky said cheerfully. He turned to his brother-in-law. "What do you think, Bernard?"

"I think I'm not getting enough pie," said Bernard, squinting worriedly down the table.

"What I'm asking is, do you think I could have a decent relationship with a woman if I wanted to?"

"No. Is there any coffee left?"

"You see, Maya," said Snooky. "Bernard understands my predicament. Besides, I think you're overrating the element of choice in our lives. What about fate?"

"What about fate?"

"Well, maybe things just happen and we can't always control them."

"You can choose who you get involved with. Somebody who runs off with someone else while she's living with you, and then writes a letter about her negative karma, is not a good choice, Snooky."

Snooky sipped his coffee, his face troubled. "That's the problem, Maya. She seemed so *right* at the time."

"You drive me crazy, Snooks. Sometimes I think you're never going to grow up."

"Oh, that reminds me. All this stuff about relationships

and settling down. Albert told me today that he and Gretchen have set a definite date. June twenty-fourth."

"That's nice."

Bernard came back abruptly from a brief, happy reverie. "June? This June?"

"That's right."

"I hope you're not planning to stay here until then?"

Snooky looked faintly insulted. "It's only five months from now, Bernard. Less than that, even. You can put up with me for that long, can't you?"

Bernard did not reply.

"I'm hurt, Bernard. I really am. But I'm not going to let it get to me, because I know that underneath that moody exterior, you're always delighted to have me around."

Bernard let out a sound like a strangled roar. He got up and left the room. After a moment, they could hear the study door slam shut.

"You're so cruel to him, Snooky," Maya said reprovingly. "You didn't mean it, did you?"

"Of course not. I already have my tickets. I'm out of here in two days. I'm going to visit some old friends in the Midwest."

"So why do you have to torture him?"

"I can't help it, My. I love watching him react. Is there any more blueberry pie, or did Bernard finish it all off before he left?"

Gretchen and Albert's wedding was held on the hottest day of the summer, in the garden of the Whitaker estate, near where the roses bloomed and the violets sent out their delicate fragrance. Gretchen wore an antique cream-colored lace dress that flattered her narrow figure, and carried a bouquet of tiny pink roses. She had tied a strip of

lace around her head, in the style of the twenties, and fastened it with a filigree brooch. She looked nervous but very happy. Albert wore a dark tuxedo and seemed to be acutely uncomfortable in it. He kept taking the jacket off in the heat, and then putting it back on. The expression of mute suffering on his face, however, gradually softened as he listened to the quiet words of the ceremony. To everyone's surprise, he managed to produce the wedding ring at the correct moment (Susan, standing next to them as the maid of honor, gave an audible sigh of relief), and, at the end, he managed to give his bride a very satisfactory kiss. Afterwards, there was a lavish garden party under yellow-and-white striped tents spread out over the lawn.

Snooky had flown in from Kansas for the wedding and was telling Maya about his current girlfriend.

"She's gorgeous, Maya, absolutely gorgeous. She's part

American Indian and she's got waist-length black hair. You've never seen anything like it. Her father was a doctor specializing in rare tropical diseases, and she's lived all over the world. She's the most fascinating person I've ever met. You should hear the stories she has to tell. We're planning to go to Burma together sometime. I feel like I've met my soul mate, Maya. My soul mate."

"I give it two weeks," Maya said, picking up an hors d'oeuvre. "Maybe three."

"You don't mean that, Maya. You say that, but you don't mean it."

"I don't like the sound of this rare tropical disease stuff. How do you know she's not carrying malaria or a parasitical worm or something?"

Snooky gazed at her reproachfully. "You're jealous. Do you realize that, Maya? You're jealous. You're always jealous of my girlfriends."

"Well, Snooky, I probably would be jealous, except none of your relationships last long enough for me to work up any real emotion over them. What do you think this is?"

"*Escabèche*," said Snooky. "Marinated poached fish. Delicious. Aunt Etta is in good voice, isn't she?"

Aunt Etta, seated at one of the tables, was calling loudly for a whisky-and-soda.

"There's Susan over there. Did you know she's been going out with that detective, what's his name, Janovy, the one who was on the case, for a couple of months now? Albert says he thinks they're getting serious. Isn't life strange?"

"Yes. Almost as strange as these hors d'oeuvres. What's this one?"

"Kappa-maki. Cucumber sushi. You dip it in the horse-radish and wrap this ginger around it."

"Oh. I see. How come you know all these things and I don't, Snooks?"

"You haven't been to as many parties as I have," said Snooky, signaling for more champagne.

Bernard was standing by the buffet table in his dull gray suit. He was sweating profusely in the late June heat and watching little Harold eating caviar.

"That's enough," he said at last. "You're not supposed to eat it with a shovel. Take one more cracker and go away."

"But I'm not done."

"You've already had more than enough."

"No, I haven't."

"Yes, you have."

"No, I haven't."

"Yes, you have."

They regarded each other with open hostility.

"What does a little kid like you know about caviar, anyway?" Bernard asked. "It doesn't seem right."

"What does a fat pig like you know about caviar?" Harold responded. "It doesn't seem right to me either."

Bernard was insulted. "I am not a fat pig."

"Yes, you are."

"No, I'm not."

"Yes, you are."

Another impasse. Bernard was struck by a wild impulse. He reached into his pocket, pulled out his wallet and thumbed out several ten-dollar bills.

"Here," he said. "I'll pay you to go away."

Harold was intrigued. "How much?"

"Thirty dollars if you'll go away and leave me alone."

"Thirty dollars," said Harold, deeply impressed. "Okay. Do you think I should tell my mother?"

"I wouldn't," said Bernard. He looked down meaningfully at Harold. A knowing glance passed between them. "I have no intention of telling my wife, or indeed anyone," said Bernard, taking a cracker and spreading it generously with black caviar. "And I suggest you do likewise."

"Gotcha," said Harold.

"Don't spend it all in one place," said Bernard, but the boy was already gone, spinning like a tumbleweed over the sunlit grass.

Bernard was sitting comfortably ensconced in his study. The lights were out and he had his eyes closed. It was the day after the wedding and he was finding it difficult to regain his concentration. Any slight interruption of his routine upset him for days, and a major social event such as a wedding could throw him off course for weeks. He was pretending now to be working, but he was actually drifting into a pleasant, dreamy reverie when the lights came on and he felt a set of tiny claws digging into his wrist.

He opened his eyes. Snooky had plopped down in the chair opposite and was grinning at him wolfishly. On Bernard's lap, clinging to his arm with all its might, was a tiny tiger-striped kitten. It bared its pointed teeth at him and began to yowl.

"Bernard, meet Snuffles Two. Snuffles, this is Bernard."

Snuffles Two was looking him over and did not seem to like what it saw. It let go of his arm and sank its teeth firmly into his thumb.

"Let go," said Bernard. "Let go. Do you hear me? Let go."

Snuffles let go. Bernard looked down at it thoughtfully. "A cat," he said.

"Correction. A kitten."

"A tiger-striped cat."

"That's right."

"And you named it Snuffles, you clever, clever bastard."

"That's right, Bernard. I hope you like the name."

"Has Maya seen it yet?"

"Oh, yes."

"And she went all misty-eyed and held it for a while and said loving things about the original Snuffles, is that right?"

"That's right. How insightful you are, Bernard."

"Then I suppose that I have no choice," Bernard said dully. At his feet, Misty growled softly.

"It's no use, Misty. We'll have to get used to it. To it, and to Snooky. He's back and he'll never leave again, will you, Snooky? This is the final visit, isn't it? The one I've been dreading all along? The one where you never, ever leave again?"

"We'll go eventually, Bernard. Don't fret. Look at Snuffles, he's crazy about you. He senses your true inner nature, your feeling of kindness and compassion toward all living beings. Isn't that right, Snuffles?"

Snuffles was curled up, purring thunderously, on Bernard's lap.

"I was just visiting Susan," Snooky said cheerfully. "She and her detective boyfriend and Harold are going to Disney World for a few days. They've been planning to go for a while, but they wanted to wait until after the wedding."

"That's nice," said Bernard. "They're taking Harold?"

"Yes."

"Well, at least he'll have some pocket money."

"What do you mean?"

"Nothing."

"Well, it's time to go." Snooky picked up Snuffles and put him on his shoulder, where the kitten clung, swaying dangerously. "Thanks for taking it so well, Bernard. See you later."

"Good-bye, Snooky."

Snooky went out, closing the door and turning out the lights, leaving a mute, defeated figure slumped in the darkness. He went downstairs to the living room and was lying on the sofa watching television when his sister came in. She picked up the kitten and began to coo.

"Oh, she's so cute, Snooky. And she looks just like my Snuffles. She really does. Just like Snuffles when I found her, years ago, when she was a kitten. Oh, she's so adorable."

"I know. Susan says even that little demon Harold took to her right away. They had never had a pet before, but he always wanted one. He calls her Mabel. Don't ask me why."

"It's hard to believe that Harold would take to anybody or anything," said Maya. "Oh, it's such a shame we can't keep her. When are they getting back from Florida?"

"Next Friday."

"Oh, well, we'll have to enjoy her while she's here. I bet Bernard was awfully relieved when you told him she wasn't staying, wasn't he?"

"Oh, yes," Snooky said. "Yes, he certainly was."

Gretchen and Albert had returned from their honeymoon and were sitting around the breakfast table on Sunday morning, reading *The New York Times*. Gretchen had the Arts and Leisure section and was going through it avidly, reading out loud.

"There's a sculpture exhibit on at the Museum of Modern Art. . . . I'm afraid I've never understood these sculptures of headless torsos and things. When it happens to Greek statues it's sad enough, but to do it *deliberately* . . . hmmmmm . . . Oh, Albert, here's that opera we've heard so much about, *Don Pasquale*. . . . They're putting it on in the park, isn't that nice? Oh, it has that new singer, Emma Kornblut. I'm sure it's going to be supercrowded, I've heard so much about her. Let's see now. It's so hot out, perhaps we'd better go to something indoors, with air-conditioning. There's a show of African art. . . . Hmmm . . . perhaps just a movie . . . hmmm . . . Oh, here, here's something nice. How about a concert? There's a new string quartet that's playing next Friday, and it sounds simply wonderful. Listen to this: Beethoven, Dvorak, Françaix—"

Albert put down his section of the newspaper and said firmly, "No string quartets."

Gretchen glanced up, and their eyes met. He leaned forward to adjust the collar of her shirt, which was sticking up. His fingers lingered thoughtfully on her neck. There was no mark left now, but the long thin red cut had bruised spectacularly and taken nearly two months to heal.

Gretchen said hastily, "Oh, yes, of course you're right, Albert. No string quartets. No string ensembles at *all*, this summer at least. Well, let's see then. . . . There's that sculpture show, as I said . . . Hmmmmm . . . twentieth-century voodoo art, I wonder what *that* is? . . . Oh, Albert, here's something you might really enjoy. . . ."

Snooky, Maya and Bernard were also sitting over the remains of their Sunday brunch. Bernard was deep into the crossword puzzle. Maya was reading one of her articles and frowning to herself.

"What's that one on, My?"

"Lizard droppings."

"Excuse me?"

"Lizard droppings. You know, spoor."

Snooky shook his head. "Who exactly buys this magazine you write for?"

"Many intelligent people, Snooky. Now shut up, I have to concentrate."

"If you wanted to concentrate, you could go to your study."

"I like working here, if you don't mind too much. It's friendlier."

"Suit yourself."

"You're just cranky because you hated to give back that kitten of yours."

"I did hate to give her back, My. I had grown very attached to Snuffles. It hurt me to give her back, especially to that subhuman vermin Harold."

"You said Harold was good with her."

"He was good with her. It was surprising. Susan says he may actually grow up to be a human being one of these days."

There was a silence.

"Snooky."

"Bernard?"

"Some help, if you don't mind. Tall flightless bird, three letters, blank M blank."

"Emu. E-M-U, Bernard."

"Oh. Okay."

Silence.

"Chinese lake, six letters, blank O blank A blank blank."

"Poyang. P-O-Y-A-N-G."

"I can never get those geographical ones," said Bernard in irritation. "One more, Snooky, if you don't mind.

Fourteen across, oracle, eight letters, blank blank N blank blank G blank T."

There was a silence.

"Oracle," mused Snooky. "Eight letters, blank blank N blank G blank blank T?"

"No. Blank blank N blank blank G blank T."

"Oracle . . . blank blank N . . . hmmmm. . . . Wait a minute, I think I have it . . . no . . . hmmmm. . . . That's a hard one, Bernard. I don't know, I'll have to think about it. Are you sure about those letters?"

"Yes."

"Hmmmm . . . all right. Let me think. No, don't look it up. Blank blank N blank blank G blank T . . . hmmmm . . ."

Snooky wandered from the room.

Maya glanced over at her husband. "That's a hard one, sweetheart. You've made Snooky happy. That'll keep him busy for hours and hours."

"It should," said Bernard. "I made it up."

Maya smiled. "You boys," she said.

THE MYSTERIOUS WORLD OF AGATHA CHRISTIE

Acknowledged as the world's most popular mystery writer of all time, Dame Agatha Christie's books have thrilled millions of readers for generations. With her care and attention to characters, the intriguing situations and the breathtaking final deduction, it's no wonder that Agatha Christie is the world's best-selling mystery writer.

☐	25678	**SLEEPING MURDER**	$3.95
☐	26795	**A HOLIDAY FOR MURDER**	$3.50
☐	27001	**POIROT INVESTIGATES**	$3.50
☐	26477	**THE SECRET ADVERSARY**	$3.50
☐	26138	**DEATH ON THE NILE**	$3.50
☐	26587	**THE MYSTERIOUS AFFAIR AT STYLES**	$3.50
☐	25493	**THE POSTERN OF FATE**	$3.50
☐	26896	**THE SEVEN DIALS MYSTERY**	$3.50

Buy them at your local bookstore or use this page to order.